AF435947

DRAECUS CLAN BOOK 4

DRAGON POWER

ALEXIS PIERCE

The man who has experienced shipwreck shudders even at a calm sea.
Ovid

CHAPTER ONE
RAYNE

I am a prince.

The thought hits me in the middle of the night. Serenity is asleep in the other room, surrounded by the rest of her mates. I've been restless ever since the queen bound us together, and tonight is no different. I'm in the kitchen baking a plate of brownies and a pink cake when the realization comes across me.

When I lost my name, I was cast out of my father's court. I was never high up in the line of succession, but being a prince was most of my identity at the time. I would spend weeks partying and taking the finest fae women to my bed, not a care in the world. It was a shock to everyone when I was sent on an actual mission, and less of a shock when I failed.

Now that I am bound to a princess, though, doesn't that technically make me a prince once again? I freeze in place, considering the implications. I don't have any real power, as the island that Serenity rules over has been abandoned for nearly two months now. Still, a shiver of pleasure runs through my body at the idea that I could be considered royalty.

When the oven timer dings, I snap out of my haze. None of that really matters right now. I'm not ruling in a castle, but caring for my mate whilst in hiding.

My lips curl up when I think of Serenity as my mate, though.

I plate the brownies and then pull the cake out of the oven, placing the trays on a cooling rack. The month spent in this cozy rural home has been strange. I can't help but feel on edge, which has resulted in my odd new hobby of baking. I've been using the smart TV in the living room to watch baking tutorials, and my experiments have been getting better and better of late.

"Rayne, what did you make this time?" Dylan

asks, startling me. I startle and grab hold of the nearest thing I could use as a weapon, which is, unfortunately, the cake pan I just pulled from the oven. I hiss and drop it, my skin turning an angry red.

I look mournfully at the destroyed cake that landed face-down on the ground. It was a new recipe that I was making special for Serenity.

"Sorry," Dylan says, his voice low and languid. He strides over and helps me clean up the mess. I shiver as his fingers brush against mine. He's the only one of the male dragons that will dare to stand so close to me, and even then it's rare. The rest don't trust me at all.

I shake my head, my hair flopping over my face. I should probably get it cut soon, although the way Serenity's hands pull at it painfully when we dream together is absolutely delicious. "I wasn't paying attention," I admit. "My mind was elsewhere."

"I see," Dylan says. He stands and dumps the ruined cake in the trash, not even flinching at the hot metal. He's a dragon, though, so he must not be affected by the heat. He reaches for the plate of brownies, pricking an eyebrow. "May I?"

I nod, keeping my face absolutely flat. Why is he talking to me like we're friends? Or at least, like we aren't enemies. Serenity isn't watching, so it's not like he has to pretend.

He takes a bite of the brownie, then groans. I lean back against the counter, pleased at the sound of approval. "This is the best brownie I've ever had," he says before taking another bite. "You got this good in a month?"

I shrug. I'm not used to praise from these men, and I'm not totally sure what type of response I'm supposed to give him. "I don't need to sleep like the rest of you. I get bored."

Dylan nods and takes a final bite, finishing off the dessert. "Well, you're really good. You could definitely give Liam a run for his money."

I frown. "I don't do it to compete with anyone."

Dylan shakes his head, cracking a smile. For someone who can suck the life out of others with a single touch, he's fairly jovial. How can that be? "I didn't mean it like that. I just meant to say that the food is good."

I nod. Having such a casual conversation is totally beyond my abilities. It's been years since I had any friends. Is that what Dylan wants from me? Friendship? I shove my hands in the pockets of my jeans, the scratchy denim irritating my skin. I hate human clothing, but there's nowhere for me to get properly-made fae attire. "Thank you." I look to the ground.

"Mind showing me how to cook something?" Dylan asks after an awkward silence. I look back up to him, surprised to find him blushing.

I tilt my head. "I don't know many recipes."

He shrugs. "I don't know any. And I've been having a really tough time since…" He trails off, looking out the window into the darkness beyond.

Ah. Serenity has told me about him when we're in private. His bloodlust is unmatched, and she's banned him from killing since an incident with hunters in the past. He needs something to keep him occupied. I can relate to that feeling.

"We could remake that cake," I say, gesturing toward the trash. For the recipe I'm following, I need several layers of the pink spongy substance, and now I only have the one cooling on the rack.

Dylan nods, a shuddering breath coming out of him. Is it really that difficult for him? For me, killing has always been a horrible task, an undertaking I've been forced into. Just the sight of blood makes me queasy, yet I've spent the better part of the past three decades as an assassin for Torres, the leader of the hunters.

I walk him through the steps, showing him how to sift flour and mix ingredients properly.

He takes to it fairly well, and we soon get into a rhythm, working around each other in a comfortable quiet.

By the time morning comes, the cake is fully decorated and the plate of brownies has been devoured. He laughs when I pull another brownie tray out of the fridge, these ones made of darker chocolate and filled with walnuts. If Serenity hates the cake, at least I know she'll like the brownies. She's been insatiable for a while now, eating all the sweets I can bake.

"Smart," Dylan says, stealing one brownie from the tray before I can stop him. It's a corner piece, Serenity's favorite. I frown, but he merely laughs at me.

It isn't long after the sun rises that the others begin to filter in. Serenity is last, just after Adrian, and I'm nearly finished doing a deep clean of the kitchen when she arrives. She wraps her arms around my waist, and I freeze, my heart fluttering in my chest at her touch.

"Morning," she mumbles, pressing her face against my back. She smells like sex, and I have to hold my breath. My cock twitches, and I have to think about baking to keep from turning around and taking her right here in front of everyone. So far, we've only been together once outside our shared dreamscape, and I want nothing more than to have her again.

"Good morning, Serenity," I say, my voice stiff and formal. I brace my hands on the counter and breathe, careful to not inhale her scent. Her hands flutter down my chest, her touch feather-light and driving me mad. When her hands brush absent-mindedly over my cock, I suck in a breath. "The others," I hiss. Although the kitchen is somewhat secluded from the living area where the drag-ons have gathered, I can't help but imagine what might happen if any of them were to walk in on us. I may be bound to her just like they are, but will that matter? Or will they kill me out of un-controllable rage?

"You're overthinking everything," Serenity sighs, pulling away from me. Despite my cau-tion, the loss of her touch is like an arrow pierc-ing my heart. I turn around to finally look at her, smiling tightly.

Her golden-silver hair is tied in a loose pleat down her back, hairs sticking out every which way. She's wearing a baggy t-shirt that hangs off one shoulder seductively, and my eyes focus on her collarbone. For some reason, I want to bite that delicate spot.

She takes a step forward, and I want to back

away, but there's nowhere I can go. There is no escaping her. She wraps her arms around my waist, pressing her ear to my chest with a sigh. "Are you afraid of them?" she asks, her voice mousy. Her hands tremble against my back until she clenches them. Is she scared to hear my response? I've never known Serenity to be anything but powerful and self-assured, so this is entirely new territory for me.

"Not exactly," I say, as I cannot lie. Her grip around me tightens, so I continue speaking. "I don't think they will ever be able to trust me, and I think that may affect your relationship with them."

In reality, I don't care if Serenity's other mates like me. The fact that their disdain may affect her, though, is enough to give me pause.

She shakes her head. "That won't happen." Her voice is strong and steady once again, and I almost think that I'd been mistaken before. But no, there had definitely been the smallest bit of fear in her voice.

I bury my head in her hair, breathing her in. Ever since we came here, it's been a struggle to get moments like this to ourselves. Around the others, I'm unsure of myself, unable to bring myself to show affection. It's ridiculous, I know, but

I can't help it. I don't want them to think badly of Serenity just because of me. My mind goes back to Dylan, though, the comfortable act of baking with him. Could it be like that with all of them? Or had that been a fluke?

"I can practically hear the gears grinding in your head," Serenity says with a chuckle. Then, she faces me, those incredible icy blue eyes penetrating deep within my soul. My breathing stops once again, and when she leans up, I don't hesitate. I take her face in my hands and press my lips against hers, a sigh of contentment coming out of me.

I may be unsure of my place in this new life, but my love for Serenity is the one thing I can approach with absolute certainty. I've never felt like this with anyone in my entire life, and I've been around far longer than the rest of them.

"You taste like chocolate," she mumbles before biting my bottom lip. I suck in a breath and pull away, my blood racing with desire. I put my hands on her shoulders, and she has the audacity to pout at me.

"You're testing my self -control," I growl, watching her as she smiles up at me.

"And you made me treats, which you should know by now is a weakness." She gives me another kiss, a simple peck this time, before taking three brownies from the tray on the counter beside me. She eyes the cake, and I roll my eyes before cutting her a slice.

A throat clears, and she and I both look up to find Liam, the mind-reading ginger, leaning against the frame of the archway that leads from the kitchen to the living room. "I was going to cook breakfast," he says curtly. All the tension returns to my body in an instant, and I nod.

"I'll leave you, then," I say. I don't give Serenity another kiss no matter how much I want to. Instead, I go up to my own room and close the door behind me.

Chapter Two
Serenity

The way the rest of my men dance around Rayne is absolutely infuriating. Even Liam, the gentlest of them all, made Rayne so uncomfortable that he fled the kitchen without so much as giving me a kiss goodbye.

Liam kisses me on the forehead, giving me a pained look. "We're trying, Princess," he says. The fear and anxiety in his voice breaks my heart just a little, but I don't waver.

"Why can't you trust him?" I ask, taking another bite of the delicious walnut brownies Rayne baked for me overnight.

Liam shakes his head. "I don't know. It's just something about him. How can we be sure that he's not still working for Torres? I can't hear a single thought in his head, and Adrian can't read him."

His frustration builds, and I set down the food before taking his hands, forcing them out of fists. Liam has always been straightforward with me, something I appreciate. Even though I don't like the words coming out of his mouth, I can at least be glad for his honesty.

"No matter how the rest of you feel, I trust him," I say. "I hope that you can all trust me enough to eventually realize that there's nothing bad going on with Rayne."

Liam's eyebrows scrunch together, and his hands tighten over mine. "I'm really trying," he says, his voice rough. I lean forward and kiss him, running my tongue over his bottom lip. He groans, pulling me closer and cupping his hands around my ass, a stark reminder that Rayne still won't touch me in front of the others. Even when we're alone, his every move is hesitant and careful. Liam pulls away, sensing the turn in my thoughts. He searches my eyes, then frowns. "You know we would never purposefully do anything to hurt you, right?"

I bite my bottom lip and nod, but my heart hurts. Will things ever be normal between all of us? Just as they finally began to trust Dylan, Rayne came along and brought with him that same distrust.

"I just want it all to be okay again," I admit, my throat thick with emotion. I look away from him and toward the living room. Matthew and Adrian are speaking in low tones, their comforting voices floating toward me. Are they talking about Rayne? With this little reprieve from battle, I should really get all these issues solved. I'm a princess, for Christ's sake. I should be able to solve a little bit of tension between my mates.

Liam pulls me into his arms, pressing his face into my hair. I allow the tension to release, although I can't help but think of all the work that still needs to get done. "It will be," he says. "I promise."

A phone rings in the living room, and Adrian answers. Liam and I look at each other, then go out. The only person who has that number is Gwen, my assistant and closest friend. She usually only calls when there's an emergency, though.

"Yes, your majesty," Adrian says. The voice on the other end is too quiet for me to discern, but it's clear by his words and respectful tone that it's my mother on the other line.

I open my mouth to ask, but he puts the phone on speaker before I have to. I walk over and join him on the couch, resting my head on his shoulder. He and I had a late morning, and I flush as I wonder if the others heard my muffled sounds of pleasure as he licked and sucked at my pussy. *This is not the time to think about that,* I chastise myself.

"I will expect all of you by the end of the day," my mother's voice says on the other line, cold and powerful.

I give Matthew a questioning glance, but he seems just as confused as me.

"Yes, your Majesty," Adrian says, then hangs up. Their conversations are always brief, so I have no idea what they were discussing. He looks at me warmly, a smile lighting up the hard lines on his face. He kisses me on the forehead, wrapping an arm around my waist as if we aren't all waiting to find out why my mother called.

I pull away and prick an eyebrow. "What was that about?" I ask.

He glances at the phone, then up at the rest of the guys. Without Rayne, they're all perfectly casual and relaxed, and Adrian doesn't even hesitate to explain, "Your mother is sending a plane.

We are to meet her in New York for a meeting with several world leaders."

My heart speeds up. "Several? In New York?" Back on the island, I spent plenty of time with politicians, but it had also helped that I didn't recognize any of them. It had been a lot like playing pretend. It was easy to act like I was in control when I didn't know anybody in the room.

Adrian nods. "A few prime ministers and the Vice President," he says.

I swallow. "Of the United States?" My voice comes out as a squeak, and Adrian tilts his head.

"Serenity, you are the princess of a nation. Surely you can't be afraid of a Vice President."

My hands tremble, so I sit on them. I don't admit that my fear lies more in whether or not I'll say something super offensive and get the island nuked. I grew up in the states, in New York City, in fact, and the one thing I learned is that the leaders tend to compensate for their insecurities with bombs instead of medication. "It's fine," I breathe, my head spinning. How am I supposed to do something like this? It was only a few months ago that I was living in basically a closet in a tiny apartment, and now I'm supposed to play dress-up and convince leaders that I know what I'm doing?

Matthew comes over and sits on my other side, taking my chin in his strong hands. His hair is braided back and put up in a ponytail, and his eyes are hard on mine. "Serenity, it will be fine. We won't let this go badly. I promise."

I let out a shaky sigh, but it doesn't help. "Okay."

He presses his lips to mine softly, and I try to let the tension flow out of me, but the idea of being in a room full of powerful people intimidates me.

"Before we go, can I ask a question?" I ask. My voice is still far too high, and out of the corner of my eye, Rayne enters, leaning against the door frame. He must have heard what's going on, because he doesn't look confused, only concerned.

"Of course," Matthew says, his breath fluttering softly over my face, smelling of mint.

"Would I get in trouble for calling someone a cunt?" I don't know who all is gonna be in this meeting, but I have a bad feeling that the word might come out, or at least something similarly foul.

Matthew shakes his head and laughs. "I think that's covered under diplomatic immunity."

Chapter Three
Dylan

The private jet is the same one we rode when I flew with the guys from New York to Miami. It was such a short time ago, but it feels like a lifetime. In a way, it was. I'd still been wary of the guys, and I'd never seen a fully-shifted dragon. Hell, I didn't even know the first thing about myself.

I prod Adrian in the waist as we climb the steps, and he turns to face me.

"Hey, remember that time you kidnapped me and I just sort of went with it?" I ask, cracking half a smile. Even before I knew about the bond between us, there had been something undeniable about Adrian that drew me to him.

He smiles, his eyes crinkling around the corners. "I think kidnapping is a strong word. I like to think of myself more like a knight in shining armor."

I laugh and press a hand against his lower back. It had also been much colder when we flew out of upstate New York, and today is just plain balmy. "Pretty sure you weren't wearing armor."

When we get on the plane, Adrian buckles me in on the sofa, then sits beside me. Rayne moves toward the back of the plane, sitting on his own. My heart races with concern, but I don't dare ask him about it in front of all the guys. It would suck to get caught in some big emotional argument on a condensed tube. At least on the boat we'd had room to shift and fly away.

As soon as the plane reaches altitude, my eyes grow heavy, and I rest my head on Adrian's shoulder. Despite the past month being so low-stress, my sleep schedule has been all sorts of fucked up. It probably has something to do with all the sex I've been having with my mates, though. Just last week I was kept up for hours by Matthew and Adrian on either side of me in bed, bringing me to completion several times. Not that I'm complaining, of course.

"How about we get you in bed?" Adrian says. "There will probably be a lot of work to do when we land. It's best you take a nap."

I nod, and he unbuckles both of us, lifting me and carrying me to the back of the plane. As we reach the last seat in the corner, I put a hand on Rayne's shoulder, tightening my fingers in the soft fabric of his shirt.

Adrian stops, and Rayne looks up at me. I smile softly, my eyes drifting shut so much I have to force them to stay open.

"Come lay with me?" I ask. He looks past me to Adrian, whose hands tighten on my thighs.

"I'm not sure that's the best idea right now, Sérénité," he says, his tongue wrapping around my given name like an incantation. My heart hurts, but I release him and let Adrian take me to bed.

He sets me down, pulling the covers around me. As he's about to remove his shoes and climb in himself, I shake my head. "I think I'd like to be alone for now," I say, my heart thrumming with hurt as it calls out for Rayne.

He hesitates, opening his mouth to speak, then shuts it. His eyebrows scrunch together, and pain fills his eyes. "As you wish," he says, leaving me be.

I may have been exhausted when I got on the plane, but now, I find myself restless. I'm so used to sharing my bed that being alone is unbearable. The way Adrian had been possessive of me, though, had upset me. I want to be with all of them, and the way he's treating Rayne is no better than the way he treated Dylan before.

My eyes burn, and tears prick at the corners. I grab a pillow and bury my face in it, muffling my sadness as well as I possibly can. Are my mates mad at me for taking another? Adrian, Dylan, Liam, and Matthew all knew each other before they ever met me, but Rayne is a total stranger. Until I claimed him, they'd never even spoken with him. Perhaps it had been a mistake. Rayne doesn't seem happy, and neither do the rest of them. Even I'm miserable, as there's something that seems hopelessly unfixable between my mates.

I almost miss a soft knock at the door, but the person on the other side doesn't wait for me to answer. I keep my face hidden, unwilling to show whoever it is that I've been crying. He lies behind me, wrapping his arms around me and burying his face in the back of my neck. I choke out a sob, and he holds me tighter.

"I'm sorry," Rayne mumbles, and a shiver runs through me. Through my thick layer of emotional distress, I hadn't been able to tell who it was until he spoke. I release my pillow and turn over, wiggling to a position where I can bury my face in his chest and force my arms around him.

"Why is it going this way?" I ask, my voice muffled through his shirt. He holds me as close as he can, petting my back. I imitate his movements, running my hands along the hard muscles of his back until I reach the hem of his jeans. Right at the center, there's something growing out of the base of his spine, and I pause, pulling away to look at him.

"Don't—" he warns, slamming his eyes shut as if that's going to change anything. The skin on his face fades up into an inky black, his tattoos a deep violet. Ridges of bone grow from his cheekbones, and his teeth have elongated. He throws an inky-black hand over his face, his fingers clawed. I've only seen his true form a few times, and every time, I'd been in danger. This time, though, it's different. He's not under anyone's control, and he doesn't move toward me.

"Rayne?" I ask, timidly placing a hand on his arm. He shudders, but his appearance doesn't change. Is his emotional turmoil so heavy that he's stuck in this form?

I pull his arm away from his face, lacing our fingers together gently. My heart speeds up as I anticipate a reaction, but none comes. He doesn't say anything, just lets me touch him as he keeps his eyes shut.

"I don't want you to see me like this," he mumbles, still unable to look at me.

I place a hand on his cheek, and he flinches the tiniest bit.

"Why not?" I ask quietly.

He shakes his head. "I don't want to frighten you."

Slowly, carefully, I move forward, pressing my lips to his. He sucks in a breath, but he doesn't pull away from me.

"I think you're beautiful," I say, tracing the tip of my thumb against the bony ridge of his cheek. He sighs, his body still trembling as he allows me to explore his features. Still, he doesn't open his eyes. "Rayne, if I were afraid of you, I wouldn't be with you. I've seen you like this before."

He shakes his head as if to clear it. Then, his eyes open, a milky white color without so much as a pupil to break it up. "And I hurt you every time. At least, I tried to." His voice is husky and dry, waiting for my judgement that will never come.

I kiss him again, and, slowly, after a moment, he kisses back, his body relaxing into mine bit by bit. He doesn't change back, though I suspect that he's able to now that his mind has calmed. Instead, he lets me touch him, lets me see him the way he truly looks.

"Are you sure this is okay?" he whispers against my lips. I pull away and watch him, his features worried but no longer panicked.

"Of course it is," I say. Then, I trace my fingers down his chest until I reach the hem of his shirt. He shivers, this time with pleasure instead of fear. Then, he helps me remove the shirt. He has more tattoos across his torso, ones I've been all too eager to explore when we're making love in our dreamscape and that one time outside while we were walking through the rental home's surrounding woods. "I love you, Rayne," I say, keeping my eyes on his as my fingers move over his skin, goosebumps rising on him.

I push gently on his chest so he lies on his back, then go to straddle him, my thighs hot and trembling at the idea of being with him in person once again. He moves his clawed hands to my waist, and they shake with worry. I put my hands over his just to reassure him, then help him move over my body. His skin burns over mine, and when his thumb brushes the underside of my breast, I gasp. His face turns up toward me, those pupil-less eyes staring at me with trepidation.

I pull my shirt off in one swift movement, then fumble behind me to unhook my bra. When it's finally off, I drag his hands up to my breasts, his ash skin contrasting against my ivory. He sits up, placing slow, careful kisses on my neck, then collar, then down my breast. The ridges on his cheeks scrape over my skin, leaving an electric sensation in their wake.

I roll my hips against his, moaning with frustration as he avoids my most sensitive areas. "Rayne," I gasp, raking my nails down his back. With that, he finally takes my nipple into his mouth, wrapping his tongue around it and sucking. I buck against him, desperate for more of his touch. It's been at least a week since he last showed up in my dreams, and I'm not sure how much longer I would have been able to go without his touch.

He hardens against me, his cock positioned just right for me to rub against it. I moan when he bites down on my nipple, rolling it between his teeth hard enough to hurt but not enough to bruise. Even though he spent the morning concerned about what the others would think, he doesn't seem to care right now. Neither do I, though.

His hands move down my body, and he un-buttons my shorts before dragging them down. I have to get off of him to remove them, and he flips me onto my back, caressing me gently as he lowers me down. The motion is so quick that it makes me dizzy, and I smile up at him as he pulls my shorts down my legs, kissing as he goes ach-ingly slowly.

My core throbs with every beat of my pulse, and I close my knees together so he can't see how hopelessly wet I am after just a couple minutes of torment. He puts his hands on my knees, his claws leaving little red marks as they scrape the skin. He moves one hand and lifts my right leg by the ankle, placing it delicately on his shoulder. Then, he kisses down the inside of my lower leg, following his hand as it traces tempting patterns over my skin. When he gets to my knees again, I'm panting with desperation. He moves his hand between my thighs, the gentlest prodding open-ing me up to him.

"I want to taste you," he whispers against my thigh before biting down. I moan, my voice high and needy. I can't even bear to look at him.

There's something about his near demonic form that awakens something wicked in me, and I want to be dominated by him over and over again. I lift my hips, and he palms my sex, his fingers running through the sensitive skin along the patch of hair down there. He moves his face down my thigh slowly, torturing me just for the hell of it.

"Please," I whimper, lifting my hips as much as I can with him holding me down. His hand goes around my left thigh, his hot breath warming me as he urges me to wrap my legs around him. His lips run delicately over my slit, a sharp pain radiating through me as my body rebels against the teasing. "Rayne, please," I beg, louder this time. He places a gentle kiss against me, his lips lingering for just an instant. I cry out, the pain of this waiting too much for me to handle. Surely the entire plane can hear us by now, but I don't care. I just need him.

Finally, his tongue parts me, about as low down as he can be before running all the way up my slit, opening my wetness to him. I groan, a shudder passing through me as I finally find the tiniest measure of satisfaction from his touch. His tongue swirls around my sensitive, swollen clit, his hands grasping my thighs. His movements are slow and measured, and they will surely be my destruction. I don't know how long I can stand this, but it feels so heavenly that I want it to last forever.

Without warning, he sucks on my clit, tightening his hands on my thighs as his claws dig into my skin. I throw my head back and cry out, unable to look at him without fear of it being too much. I roll my hips, but he doesn't relent. When I look at him again, he's back to his more human form, his skin once again pale and his tattoos inky black. Amusement glimmers in his eyes, and he runs one hand down and thrusts two fingers into me without warning.

"Rayne," I cry, the feeling of him filling me while sucking overwhelming. How am I supposed to hold on much longer?

He adds another finger, spreading my walls just a little more. One finger finds the right spot while his tongue flicks over my clit, and I lose all control, wrapping my fingers in his hair and screaming out, my back arching as every muscle in my body tenses.

Instead of showing up and receding, though, the attack on my senses just keeps coming, like waves crashing violently against seaside cliffs. Every time I think it's almost over, he thrusts his fingers again and sucks against my clit, forcing it to keep going. I pant and thrust, trying to figure out how to make this end, but he just keeps going, sucking out every ounce of pleasure he can get from me.

Finally, when it's truly too much and my cunt throbs with a mixture of pain and overwhelming pleasure, he lets me go, pressing his lips against my thigh and then moving up my body. I shudder and moan, wrapping my arms around him and burying my face in his neck. My trembling is finally able to recede, and he kisses my forehead while I recover from the aftershocks.

"Fuck," I whisper, as if there's a single person on this plane who didn't hear that.

He smiles against my forehead, then moves to lie on his side. I immediately pull myself into his arms, pressing my body against his and wrapping my legs around his. I don't even bother getting dressed. The orgasm had been so intense that it wiped me out, and I fall asleep in his arms within moments.

CHAPTER FOUR
LIAM

When Serenity cries out, the sound of pleasure all too familiar, I stand up and go to the restroom toward the front of the plane. I can't stop imagining the ways Rayne could be pleasuring her, her body reacting to his the same way it has reacted to mine countless times.

My cock has hardened painfully against my jeans, and the moment the door is locked, I undo my pants and take it in my hand. I close my eyes and picture Serenity, her body contorting with pleasure. The way she smelled when she and Adrian came down this morning was nothing in comparison with the sounds she's now making, and I rub my cock as I picture her, Rayne pleasuring her the way she likes.

A pounding at the door breaks me out of my stupor, and I groan. What now?

I zip up my pants clumsily and open the door a sliver. Matthew is standing there, his eyes dark with lust. He must be having the same thoughts as me. Before I can tell him to leave me alone, he pushes into the bathroom with me. It's bigger than something from a commercial flight, but still far too small to take both of us.

"What are you—" I start, but he presses his lips to mine aggressively, and I take the opportunity to shut the hell up. I grab his hips, steadying myself in the small space.

"I can't fucking stand hearing that shit," he groans. I almost think he means that he's angry about Serenity and Rayne, but the hardness in his pants says otherwise. He's just as turned on as I am. I unbutton his pants, then hesitate before moving to the zipper. He leans back against the wall and nods, watching me as I free his length, wrapping my hand around it before beginning to pump up and down. He tilts his head back and mutters a curse.

Then, unexpectedly, he pulls my hand off of

him before undoing my pants. He grabs my hips and forces me to back up against the counter, running his lips against my neck. "I want you to fuck me in the mouth," he whispers, his voice gruff. I nod to show I understand. Then, he moves down to his knees, pulling my pants down before taking my length in his hand. When he licks his lips, I swallow, my breathing going shallow.

Is this seriously happening? Is Matthew going to suck me off in the airplane bathroom? He takes me into his mouth greedily, taking far more than I expected in one go. At this point, his thoughts assault my mind, and the way he feels while sucking my cock reflects back in my body. I pant as I grasp the countertop, and he moans, his throat vibrating around me. I thrust my hips, gently at first as he adjusts to my girth. The longer it lasts, though, the more of me he takes, moaning every time I thrust into him. The soreness of his stretching lips is what makes it so sweet for him, and I wrap one hand below his jaw.

He moves a hand to his pants, jerking himself off while he sucks me. All of the physical sensations running through me are too much, pleasure bursting through me uncontrollably. "I'm going to—" I gasp, trying to do the right thing and pull away, but he only takes me further, tightening his throat and tongue around me as I gasp out and finish inside him, coming hard and fast.

He moans and releases me, his body shuddering as he finds his own climax. He gasps and moans against my hip bone, and I throw my head back as I relish in our mutual pleasure. Can he feel it, too? After all, he's able to feel others' physical injuries when he's touching them. Maybe he felt everything he was doing to me the same way I do.

"Fuck," I say with a breathless laugh. It's been a while since Matthew and I have done anything together, and I forgot how good it can be with him. I'm still the only man he's been with, as he and Adrian still have yet to work out their feelings for each other. No matter how much I try to talk to him about it, though, Matthew always closes up when it comes to that particular subject.

Matthew stands up and cleans himself up, and I leave him be. Adrian is watching me when I leave, the tiniest bit of jealousy burning in his eyes. Oh, well. If he wants Matthew, then they will have to work it out between themselves. I'm not going to deny myself what I want just because they can't communicate with each other.

I go to one of the armchairs and buckle up, leaning my head back and closing my eyes. It seems that whatever Serenity and Rayne were doing is over, at least, so I won't have to deal with that added arousal for the rest of the plane ride. When Matthew walks in, his feet shuffle to one of the seats nearer the back of the plane, and I allow myself to drift off.

ADRIAN

Maybe I was wrong about Matthew. For years, I've felt something between us. At least, I thought I did. Now, though, my mind is a jumble as I wonder why he always goes to Liam instead of me. We spoke briefly about our feelings once, but we agreed that it would best to just be friends while everything is going on. Matthew promised he'd talk to me when things settled, though.

I frown as Liam exits the bathroom. This doesn't seem to be settling. Before Matthew comes out, I lean back and feign sleep. First Serenity asks me to leave her alone, and then Matthew goes and has sex with Liam. I shouldn't be angry, but all of this is just getting frustrating. I don't need to bother the others with these emotions, though. It's not their fault I'm feeling neglected. I need to deal with my jealousy issues myself. Preferably by punching something.

As the plane prepares to land, Serenity and Rayne emerge from the bedroom. She's clearly just woken up, her eyes still thick with sleep. She kisses him on the cheek, and a pang of irrational fear runs through me. I have no reason not to trust Rayne, but every time I think of him with Serenity, I picture the time she almost bled to death in my arms because of him, and there was nothing I could do to stop it. I told her over and over again that she was going to be okay, but I wasn't even sure I believed it. Logically, I know that it was Torres' command that made Rayne do it. However, everything in my body screams at me that this man is dangerous.

The plane lands smoothly on the runway, rain pattering down on the windows. The private terminal at LaGuardia is far from the rest of the airport, and I take Serenity's hand and lead her down to the black stretch limousine with Draecus Island flags on the antenna.

Serenity is the first one in, and she lies down with her head in my lap as soon as I move next to her. She slept for a large portion of the plane ride, so how is she still so tired? I rest the back of my hand on her forehead. Her temperature feels normal, but concern still roils through me.

I frown at Matthew, and he nods. He'll look at her when we're safely in our hotel room. When the car starts to move, my body is put back on edge. We've been in hiding for a while, and now we're being paraded around in the most obvious car in the world. It would be far too easy for a rebel or hunter to attack us.

Nothing happens on the ride, though, and the car pulls to the rear entrance of the hotel. I wake Serenity, and she looks around blearily. Her aura is filled with confusion, and I stroke her face with one hand. "It's alright princess. We just got to the hotel."

She nods, and the five of us lead her out of the car and into the hotel, serving as bodyguards. Her fingers twine through mine as I walk ahead of her, shoulder-to-shoulder with Liam.

We take the service elevator to the penthouse suite on the very top floor. The doors open to reveal four faces we haven't seen in months.

Serenity stiffens, her hand squeezing mine almost painfully.

"Mom," she says, moving up to stand beside me.

CHAPTER FIVE
SERENITY

Adrian releases my hand, and my four dragon mates bow at the appearance of my mother and her mates. Rayne copies them awkwardly, clearly uncomfortable with the procedure.

"Serenity," my mom, Queen Amelie, says, opening her arms and stepping toward me. I rush forward and wrap myself in her arms, tears pricking at my eyes. The last time I saw her in person was when the castle was being attacked by rebels. Despite seeing her on TV and talking on the phone, there was still a small part of me that thought it was all a trick.

"It's good to see you again," Henri, one of her mates, says, approaching Adrian and grasping his forearm in a formal handshake. I pull away from my mother and watch the interaction. I knew that Adrian was close with the royal family, but seeing them reunite is like seeing family together again for the first time.

"Serenity, you seem well," Phillip says, stiff and formal as always. I haven't spent much quality time with my mom and her mates, so despite knowing them for a while, I'm uncomfortable around them. How am I supposed to act around the people who were supposed to be my parents but sent me away?

I nod. "I am. The past month has been a good respite from battle." My words are just as formal and stiff, and I feel like I'm putting on an act. In reality, the past month has been just as exhausting as all the time we spent tracking down hunters. Dealing with the cacophony of emotions between my mates has been a lot to handle.

Tomas, my biological father, comes forward and wraps his arms around me. He's the only one of the three I've been around much, and his reception is warmer than I expected. After a moment of not knowing what to do, I return the hug. Is this what a father's love is supposed to feel like? My adoptive father was always kind to me, but he kept his distance. Tears prick at my eyes, and I have to pull away before I start crying.

"And you must be Rayne," Mom says, opening her arms to welcome my newest mate. He steps forward awkwardly, hands shoved in his pockets when she pulls him into an embrace. He looks at me pleadingly, and I stifle a laugh. Is this what it's like for girls with normal families to bring home their boyfriends?

I look around the room, noting how all of my mates other than Rayne seem far more comfortable than they have in months. I smile, crossing my arms in front of my chest.

"So," I say, "what's the plan?"

Over the next few days, I'm introduced to dozens of people who are tasked with turning me into a proper diplomat. I cry out and pull Hans into my arms when he's led into my private room in the penthouse. He was my hair and makeup artist back at the palace, and I was never certain if he and his mate made it out safely. He then proceeds to chastise me for the state of my hair.

"Just because you're a refugee doesn't mean you shouldn't deep condition," he says. "And what about that seven step Korean skincare routine? Your skin is practically scaly."

I laugh at his stern evaluation. "I am a dragon," I remind him, and he gasps at my nonchalance.

"This is a serious matter," he says, grabbing a suitcase and getting to work making me presentable.

I've asked about Gwen returning, but nobody seems able to give me a straight answer. Having my mates for support is wonderful, but there's something about having a girl friend that I just don't get from being surrounded by nearly half a dozen men.

"It's too tight," Matthew complains from the other side of my bed, where a tailor is doing his final fitting for a new suit. All of my mates are getting tailored clothing, but Matthew is the one who hates it the most. Still, I can't deny that the suit looks incredible on him. The four of them are going to be wearing all-black suits, and I lick my lips at the sight of Matthew in his formal attire. He turns his eyes up to me and gives a pained smile.

"It's supposed to be snug," the tailor says, his Italian accent muffled over the pins in his mouth.

"You don't want to look like you're wearing something off the rack."

Matthew gives a look of mock horror. "Not off the rack. How ever will I live?"

I snicker, leaning my head back as Hans applies some sort of fancy skin cream. "This will help with the dryness and have you practically glowing," he says.

Our meeting with the nations' leaders is in just a few days, and every time I think about it, it sends my heart racing. How am I supposed to act like I know anything about world policy with these people? Just a few months ago I was a minimum wage employee at a college's media center.

"You'll be meeting with the British, Canadian, and Italian Prime Ministers, as well as the Vice President of the United States and the President of Mexico. Your meeting with the European Union is next week, and we're trying to set up something with China, Japan, South Korea, and India," Henri says. Mom is out doing her own important meetings, and Henri has been in charge of bringing tutors and informing me of all my upcoming responsibilities.

"And what about all the other countries," I ask, half joking and half panicking. I have no idea how to speak with these people.

He navigates to another page on his iPad, then continues listing meetings with other nations. My hands shake, so I grip the leather arms of the salon chair hard. "It looks like Russia wants to have you there, so we're working on scheduling flights. You'll also be attending the UN assembly in September. We believe that we have a good case for Draecus Island joining the UN, so you and your mother will be going together."

I nod, all the information overloading my brain. All I'm really hearing is that I have to talk to a bunch of career politicians like I know what I'm doing. Will I be the one to screw it all up for my people? Where most of these people have their whole lives to prepare for these roles, I've had less than half a year.

When Hans begins to massage some sort of oil into my hair, my eyes drift shut, Henri's words blurring together into a big blob of meaningless chatter.

"Serenity?" Matthew asks, and I snap my eyes open. He's leaning over my chair, Henri, Hans, and the tailor standing back. I blink at him, then lift a hand to smooth out the concern pushing his eyebrows together.

"What's up?" I ask, smiling. I must have fallen asleep in the chair.

He frowns back at me. Did I do something wrong? "You fell asleep in the chair half an hour ago. You've been sleeping a lot lately. I'm just a bit worried about you. I think I should examine you to make sure there's nothing wrong."

He looks up at the others, and they immediately file out in order to give us some privacy.

"I'm okay," I say, sitting up and stretching. "It's just been a lot to deal with, you know?"

He nods. "Can I still look? Just to be sure?"

Now that I really evaluate him, he almost seems frightened. I sigh and nod. "I guess there's no harm in it."

I stand up and walk over to the bed, lying down on my stomach. Matthew removes his suit jacket and joins me on the bed, hesitant. I pat my ass. "Sit here," I mumble, sinking into the mattress. "You should give me a back rub while you're at it."

Matthew's laugh is quiet, but definitely there. Pride swells in my heart, and he does as I say, straddling me and resting right at the base of my butt. His hands run under my shirt, applying a deep pressure that drags a moan out of me. I had no idea how tense I was until he started touching me.

"That feels nice," I groan. He chuckles, and a

warmth spreads from his hands over my back.

"I'm just checking your body for anything un-usual," he says, his magic flowing through me like a hot bath. I grunt in acknowledgment.

He moves his hands up my back, massaging as he works his magic through me. When he's finished, my eyes have drifted shut once again. He climbs off of me, then leans against the head-board. "Serenity, are you asleep again?" he asks. The concern is gone, leaving only amusement. He must have finally accepted that there's noth-ing wrong with me.

I shake my head, and his hand rests in my hair, moving through and massaging my scalp. It isn't long before I drift right back into a dreamless sleep. The meetings might go fine, but I might also just fall asleep in the middle of them.

CHAPTER SIX
SERENITY

I'm wearing my own tailored suit for the meeting, a dark magenta color with a Draecus pin on the lapel. I didn't even know those were made. I'm sitting on the plane with Mom and all our mates. It's a short hop from New York to Washington, D.C., and my leg shakes the whole time.

Liam puts a hand on my thigh, and I pause to look at him. He smiles. "It's going to be alright," he says.

I nod, but I'm not totally sure I believe him. When the plane lands, I stand up as straight as I can. They tried to put me in a pair of high heels, but I don't want to fall on my face in front of several world leaders, so I'm in a more sensible pair of loafers.

When we exit the plane, I'm surprised to find that, instead of an airport, we've landed at an Air Force base. Another plane rests on the tarmac nearby, a sleek black jet with the Canadian flag on the tail.

Just as I was warned, there's a whole fleet of photographers behind a chained-off area, and their cameras start clicking the moment I step through the door. My mother will be the last off the plane, as she's the most important one. Still, having to walk down the steps while a dozen reporters call my formal name, Sérénité.

Adrian leads me down, and I take his hand as I reach the final step. When I reach the ground, I release him. All of my men are here for me, looking more like bodyguards with their black suits and bluetooth earpieces. I guess that's their role for now, though. Even Rayne is dressed to the nines, his tattoos expertly covered by Hans and his makeup kit.

"Princess Sérénité, who are you wearing?" a woman with a notepad says as the photographer next to her flashes a camera. The question throws me. I've been expecting questions on my domestic and foreign policy ideas, but instead they just want to know who made my suit. I keep a placid smile on my face and ignore the question.

"Princess Sérénité, the internet is calling you the hottest princess of the century, and readers want to know if you're single."

Jesus fucking christ. I refuse to sway at this line of questioning, and I loop my arm through my mother's when she reaches the base of the stairs. Our men walk behind us and to the side, and, through her teeth, she says, "This is why I didn't want to go public. This misogyny is unbearable."

I chuckle, making sure my face stays exactly the same. The reporters shout similar questions, but we walk straight to the black SUV and climb in, Tomas holding the door for us. He and Adrian are the only ones to ride in our car, and the rest of our mates follow in the second. I can't help but worry about them, wondering if they're safe.

When we leave the base, though, the sight makes me balk. We aren't just driving through Washington DC, but the streets have been completely cordoned off for our arrival. Side streets are blocked by barriers and police cars, so it's a straight shot from the Air Force base to the White House.

I can't believe I'm actually going there. I watch

in disbelief as we go through the gate, then park in a special area just for us. There's press here, too, but they're less excitable than the ones at the base. They stand back and take their photos, but they don't try to ask questions. Mom and I walk into the building together, escorted by our men as well as secret service agents, at least that's what I assume by their attire.

I'm not sure what to expect, but when we walk into an ornate sitting room, I pause. There's hardly anyone in here at all, and the men with us spread around the room, flanking the doors. One man has a camera around his neck, but otherwise there are only a few others, all of which I recognize from the news and memes.

The Vice President is the first to greet us. "Queen Amelie and Princess Sérénité, it's lovely to meet you," he says. He holds a hand out and shakes each of ours in turn, his smile too bright and white hair slicked so much that not a strand is out of place. The cold look in his eyes sends a shiver down my spine, and I might squeeze just a bit too hard. He pulls away with a wince. "Hell of a handshake you've got there," he says, flexing his hand.

I give a halfhearted laugh, glad when the next person moves. It's the handsome Canadian Prime

Minister, and his smile seems warm and genuine. "Great meeting you," he says. "I'm so excited to learn about your country."

I smile back and give him a normal handshake. "Thank you, Prime Minister," I say. "I've always admired many of Canada's policies, although I will say your Indigenous Rights are lacking." His smile tightens just a hair, and I can see that I've gotten to him.

Stop talking, Serenity, my brain screams. I glance over to see amusement twinkling in Dylan's eyes, and an ounce of disapproval in Adrian's.

The next to shake my hand is the Mexican President, and he's clearly wary. I shake his hand, refusing to say anything, although I'm half tempted to blurt out asking why he capitalized on a pandemic. I resist, though.

When the British Prime Minister approaches, I grit my teeth and bear it. "Prime Minister," I say as politely as I can muster for such a sleaze ball, which isn't very polite at all. If my words were filled with venom, he would have been hit with a lethal dose.

The Italian Prime Minister is the last to introduce himself. Italy is the nearest country to Draecus Island, so I really shouldn't offend the Prime

Minister. "Thank you for all your assistance regarding Draecus Island refugees," I say.

He smiles. "Nothing less for our mysterious neighbors."

Adrian gives me a pained expression. I fucked the meeting up, but not irreparably. Mom takes the lead from there, and I spend most of my time listening.

"Serenity, I've heard that you were trying to pass a Basic Income in your nation's parliament before the attacks?" the Canadian Prime Minister says, folding his hands together and leaning his forearms on his knees.

My heart stutters. It had been hotly debated by my own people, and the idea of the world having it under scrutiny is so much more intimidating.

"That's right," I say. "Based on research, it seems that a Universal Basic Income from birth would reduce poverty rates, and poverty is generally one of the largest reasons for political unrest."

The British minister frowns. "But how will paying people off stop the rebellions you clearly can't control?"

I set my jaw and look him square in the eye. "It's not paying people off. It's a long term solution to ensure that every citizen in my country has a fair chance at life, no matter what their status is at birth."

The Vice President nods, clearly just humoring me. "But aren't you concerned about people spending the money on drugs and alcohol? How can you trust the poor to do the right thing with that money?"

I smile at him sweetly, my words like ice. "First of all, studies of similar programs have pointed to the contrary. Basic wages boost economies and ensure that people aren't starved when automation takes over their industries, and it also eliminates wage slavery. But I wouldn't expect you to understand, since your country's economy thrives on the broken backs of the poor." I turn back to the rest as the photographer snaps his camera. I ignore the lens and continue my tirade. "On Draecus Island, we believe in investing in our citizens. Districts with UBI have higher education rates, lower poverty rates, and since it would be available to all citizens regardless of income, it encourages upward mobility instead of trapping lower-income citizens in cycles of welfare dependence."

The condescending looks from the men in the room who proclaim to be able to lead nations is infuriating. My mother, her mates, and my mates, however, look at me with pride. I may not be able to impress these leaders, but from the moment I landed in Washington, D.C., I knew that I wouldn't be respected simply because of my gender. This room is no different. These men, barring the Italian Prime Minister, all live in countries where they treat the lowest-class citizens with disdain, and I'm just a silly little girl who has even sillier ideas.

I stand up and hold my hand out to shake that of the Italian Prime Minister. "It was lovely meeting you, and I look forward to speaking more in the future."

He grins. "We'd love to have you in Italy any time."

To the rest of the men, I say, "Thank you for having me," then stride out of the room. My men follow me, and so do my mother and her mates.

As soon as Mom and I are back in our black SUV, she looks at me, her expression unreadable. "Holy shit, Serenity," she says, the words harsh and unexpected below her thick Draecus accent. I'm not sure exactly what she means by that until she continues, "It was quite the sausage-fest in there, as they say in the states. But I think you did alright."

When we pull into the Air Force base to return

to New York, Henri's iPad is blowing up with news and Twitter notifications. He frowns.

"What does it say?" I ask, holding my hand out for the iPad. He hesitates, but one glance at my mom's face is enough that he passes it over.

Princess Snubs Leaders, the headline reads. The White House pictures have been shared all over the world already, and different news outlets have different opinions. I read through a few, but they're so varied that it doesn't really matter. I shrug and pass the device back.

"Some people aren't going to like me," I say simply. "I'm not going to stop helping people just because some dudes who think they're smarter than me disagree with my policies."

Mom's hand lands on my shoulder, and her eyes twinkle with pride. "You're doing wonderfully," she says, her voice filled to the brim with emotion.

I smile. "Thanks."

CHAPTER SEVEN
DYLAN

I'm the first one on the plane, and I hold my hands behind my back, waiting for Serenity. We organized a surprise for her, and when she gets on the plane, the young woman in the back room leaps through the door.

"Gwen!" Serenity says, running over to hug her best friend. "I missed you so much! How did you get here?"

She pulls away, and Gwen explains how she had to get so many special clearances just to get to us, starting with the fact that she didn't have her passport when she fled the island. It took a lot of work just to get her here today. "I was supposed to meet you when you landed, but we were delayed because of the motorcade. I'm so happy to see you!"

They spend the whole flight chattering about the news, and Gwen laughs at the way Serenity treated the presidents and prime ministers. "I mean, it's not a crime to be a dick," Gwen says.

Serenity snorts. "They might make a new law just for me."

The plane takes off, and I watch Liam, who's avoided talking to me for a while. He's been distant since we started going on missions to take out hunters, and I can't deny that it hurts a bit. I want to tell him how shitty I feel about it all, but he has been carefully avoiding me, ensuring that we aren't even alone in a room together.

After landing back in New York, he rides in a separate car with Serenity and Gwen, while I ride in the queen's car. I nod at the guards who've been hired to secure the perimeter. This hotel is filled with high-profile paranormal clientele, which means that they have very stringent security measures to protect those inside. That's why the queen chose it. Nobody gets in or out without clearance, and it's physically impossible to cause harm to another within its structure because of all the spells it's under. As soon as we walk inside, it's like a hollowness has been carved out of my chest. Due to the nature of my powers, the building completely buries them within me every time I come in.

"I think I need a nap," Serenity says when we make it to the penthouse where we've been staying the past week. She says goodbye to Gwen, and I lift her into my arms so that she doesn't fall on the ground and sleep there. "Thank you, Dylan," she mumbles into my chest. I tighten my hold on her, warmth filling me.

Rayne follows us to the bedroom. Ever since we showed up in New York, he and I have grown more comfortable with each other. The others may think he's a monster, but they thought the same of me. As far as I'm concerned, if he's her mate, he can be trusted.

"Is she doing alright?" he asks, concern etched in his features when I lay her down and tuck the blankets around her. He brushes his hand through his hair, and I can't help but notice once again how his hands look just a little wrong, a little less than human.

"Yeah, it's just a lot for her, I think," I say, but I'm still concerned. Matthew checked her out and didn't find anything, and I trust him to know better than anyone else. Still, the frequency of Serenity's sleeping is concerning. "You aren't hanging out in her dreams and keeping her from getting rest, are you?" That's what was going on before, but even on nights where he's definitely awake, Serenity doesn't seem to get enough sleep.

He shakes his head. "No. I haven't been sleeping. I know it wears her out."

Serenity's eyes blink open, and she looks up at the two of us. "Come to bed," she says, reaching a hand out.

I smile and join her, and Rayne looks like he might flee.

"Where are you going?" I ask. "There's plenty of room."

He hesitates, evaluating me. "The rest of them don't trust me."

I shrug, and Serenity curls up against my side, her heat comforting. "That's what they thought of me, too. They'll just have to get used to the fact that you're not going anywhere." I don't mention that Liam still avoids me, or how much it hurts to feel like an outsider even after knowing them for so long.

He frowns, but he removes his suit jacket and folds it over a chair before lying on Serenity's other side. Carefully, like I might strike him, he puts a hand in her hair, scratching her scalp in slow, gentle patterns.

She groans against me. "That's nice," she mumbles before falling into a nearly instant sleep.

I shake my head. "I'm worried about her, too. Matthew can't find anything wrong with her, but there's something different about this. You know?"

He nods. "I think so. She had more energy when we were first bound. Do you think…" He stops speaking, though, staring at nothing.

I watch him. "Do I think what?"

He frowns again. "Do you think it's my fault? That my presence is causing it?"

I shake my head. "I really don't."

He sighs, relief flooding out of him.

I nuzzle my face in Serenity's hair, taking in a deep breath filled with her scent. "I'm gonna get some sleep. Wake me up if anything happens."

MATTHEW

I lie on the bed in the extra bedroom, the one where Rayne has been sleeping as far as I know. I run my hands through my hair, frustration building in me. Serenity is just as tired as ever, and now she's in the other room with Dylan and Rayne. I've used my powers to check her several times this week, but every time I come up with nothing. I can't feel anything wrong with her that could be making her so damn tired.

I throw my arm over my face, groaning. The door opens, and I jerk up to see who's disturbing me.

"Sorry," Adrian says, moving to close the door. "I thought this room was free."

"Wait," I say just as he's almost gone. My stomach rolls with indecision. "It's cool. If you want to hang out in here."

The words come out awkward, and I scoot over on the bed and cover my face once again. Being around Adrian stirs up all sorts of strange feelings inside me, and right now is no different. With Liam, it's easy. I enjoy fucking him, and he seems to reciprocate those feelings. Adrian is different, though. We've been friends for so long that I don't know what would happen if we were to hook up. It could ruin everything.

Still, I can't help but remember the kiss right before the bonding ceremony. The way his lips had met mine, desperate and hungry, and the way I kissed him back. Devine.

Adrian comes over to the bed and lies down as well, staying right against the edge away from me. Maybe my lack of action has already done enough to ruin anything we might have had.

"It seems like things have calmed down for now," I mumble after a long, awkward silence.

I uncover my face and peek at Adrian, who is watching me carefully, like I'm an animal who will bolt at the slightest provocation.

Hell, I still might. My heart thumps so loud that the whole suite can probably hear it even through the sound-proof walls.

"Seems like it," Adrian says, clearly unsure of my intentions.

I turn to face him, propping my head up on my hand. "Did I ruin everything?" I finally ask, the question that has been bothering me for weeks. "I know I said we'd talk about things, but then I sort of just…stopped talking."

He turns to mimic my position, his dark eyes careful. "I don't think I know what you mean."

I bite my lip in frustration. I don't want to be the one to say it, but it seems like that's the way it's gonna have to be.

"I don't know if you still have…feelings," I say, my words halting, "but I do. And I wanted to maybe discuss that. With you."

CHAPTER EIGHT
ADRIAN

Matthew still has feelings for me? My heart pounds like it's trying to break out of my chest. I sit up slowly, and he does the same so we're sitting across from each other on the bed.

"And by discuss, you mean…?" I ask. I don't want to make any assumptions, but hope blooms in my core anyway. I could be reading this whole thing wrong, and putting too much pressure on this one thing could break me.

Matthew looks at his hands, his shoulders hunching.

"Goddamn it, Adrian, do I need to spell it out

for you? I'm in love with you, okay? I have been for a long fucking time, and—"

I cut him off, slamming my lips against his. I have to kneel and wrap my hand around the back of his neck, holding him tight. After the initial shock wears off, his icy demeanor melts, and he kisses me back. Being connected to him after so much time away is like getting water in a desert.

He puts one hand on my cheek, running his thumb over my stubbled jawline. Slowly, he pulls me down, his body flat against the bed. I put a knee on either side of his thighs, relishing the feeling of our bodies pressed together.

I pull my lips from his and trail them along his jaw, then to his neck. I unbutton the first button of his dress shirt, then the second. Shakily, he undoes the rest so that I can run a hand over the tight muscles of his chest.

Matthew tangles a hand in my hair as I kiss him, and his hips thrust against me softly, like he's doing it subconsciously.

I bite down on his nipple, and a small cry comes out of his throat as his hand tightens, pulling my hair painfully. My cock hardens at the sensation, and I grip his hip bone hard enough that it may bruise.

"Adrian," Matthew groans, and I look up at

him, he watches me, his eyes dark as he traces his other hand over my face, his fingers running over my mouth. I part my lips, my body still as his first finger dips into my mouth. I run my tongue over the tip, and he sucks in a breath. My body hums with electricity, the simple act of taking Matthew's finger into my mouth one of the greatest sensations of my life.

A whine pulls itself out of my throat, my lust growing too great to handle. I release Matthew's finger, then move my lips down his chest, then over his stomach until I reach the waistband of his slacks. With nimble movements, I unhook his pants and caress his cock, running my thumb over the tip until a small dot of precum comes out.

Then, my eyes flicking up to his for an instant, I take him into my mouth, and he groans, leaning his head back. The sensation of his cock in my mouth is new, stretching my lips in an unexpected way. I experiment with taking more of him in, and one of his hands runs through my hair, his hips rolling gently.

I groan as he fills my mouth, my cock throbbing with need when he gasps. Need devours me, and I reach down to stroke my own cock straining against my pants.

Matthew clenches his hand in my hair, dragging me off him with a sweet sort of pain. His eyes are aflame as he breathes in the scent of us together.

"I need to fuck you," he growls, and my cock twitches.

"Yes," I whisper, staying perfectly still while he evaluates me. When he lets me go, I move to his side, my hands straying up his chest.

He bites his bottom lip, his teeth slightly sharper than usual. He sits up slowly, watching me hungrily as he reaches into the lone drawer of the bedside table. I suck in a breath when I see the tube of lubricant he's holding, my body quivering with anticipation.

"Take off your shirt," he says, his voice rough. I do as he says, my skin lighting with electricity when it's exposed to the cool air. His chest heaves as he sets the lubricant down, his hand reaching toward me of its own volition. I take it, our skin hot against each other, and rest his fingers against the pounding heart trying to escape my chest. His touch is so tentative and gentle, a stark contrast to the gruff man I've fallen in love with over the past few years.

His eyes flick down, and I help his hand move down to the waist of my pants. He doesn't hesitate to undo them, and I remove them after. His nostrils flare as he appraises my entirely exposed form. "Lie down," he orders, his voice shaking.

A bolt of electricity pins me, and I follow his instructions slowly, my eyes on his the whole time. I lie on my back, and he joins me on his side, his hand trailing up and down my body.

"We don't have to," I mumble, watching his expression closely.

His eyes flick up to mine. "I want to." After a pause, he asks, "Do you?"

I nod, then reach a hand up to caress his cheek. He leans down and presses his lips to mine, his cock pressing against my hip. His every movement is careful, calculated. I let him go as slowly as he needs.

He pulls his lips away, his breath hot and minty across my face. "Will you turn on your side?"

I do as he asks, and his body shivers against mine. I lean my head back, and he places the softest of kisses against my neck. His hand strays down my waist, over my hip, and his fingers reach my entrance. He fumbles for the lube, and I wait patiently, my every muscle taut in anticipation. When he finds my entrance again, his fingers are slick and cool.

"Is this alright?" Matthew asks, his lips brushing over my ear.

"Yes," I breathe, and he bites down on the sensitive lobe. Heat rushes to the spot, a stark contrast to the cold of his fingers as he parts me, working my tight hole open slowly. A groan rumbles out of my chest. I take in a deep breath to steady myself, forcing my body to relax as he works me. My hand flies down to my cock, stroking it as Matthew prepares me. His lips trail over my throat, and I lean back against him, his chest hot as a furnace against my back.

"Are you ready?" he asks, his voice gruff and unsteady.

I close my eyes and breathe out through my nose. "Yeah," I breathe, working my thumb over my wet tip.

He removes his fingers, which are quickly replaced by his cock nudging at my entrance.

"I need you to take the lead here," Matthew says, his tip working into me. For an instan, the stinging as I stretch open throws me off. I suck in a breath, reaching my free hand under my head to tangle in his hair and steady myself. I rock against him, adjusting to his thickness. Slowly, I push myself closer, his cock gliding into me.

"Matthew," I gasp, releasing my own cock to grab his hand on my waist.

He freezes. "Do I need to stop?"

I shake my head, closing my eyes while my skin tingles all over. I guide his hand to my cock, groaning when he grips it and starts pumping.

As my body relaxes, I take him in further, all the way until he's seated inside me. I twist my head against him, my lips finding his as my core hums with a sort of rightness. He kisses me roughly, keeping himself steady. I roll my hips back, and he presses further against me, our bodies flush.

Slowly, I pull away, then push back against him. He follows my movement, sliding in and out at a measured pace. With every thrust inward, I gasp. With my entire body alight, it isn't long before I can feel my completion coming. I shudder and surrender, a shout climbing out of me before I can stop it. He holds me tight as I finish in the sheets, and it isn't long before he's joining me, his aura lighting up like a power grid as he bucks against me.

"Adrian," he groans, pressing his face into my neck and gasping, his body straining against mine. I clench around him, riding him through his own orgasm.

As his trembling slows, he pulls out of me, his cock twitching against me as he exits. I turn onto my back, turning my gaze back to him. All the turmoil from the past months settles inside me for the first time, leaving me with a level calm as I see him anew.

I reach a hand up and trace his lips.

He's mine. He always has been, and he always will be.

CHAPTER NINE
SERENITY

It's still the wee hours of morning when I wake up. I find Rayne and Dylan still asleep in bed beside me, so I'm careful to get up and climb out before they can even notice that I'm awake. Despite the fact that I slept for at least twelve hours, my body isn't groggy in the slightest. Instead I feel wound up and energized, so I need something to get this energy out. I've heard that the hotel has a gym somewhere so when I exit the bedroom, I grab a key card off of the table next to the door. Then I exit the room and head towards the elevators.

"Hold the door!" someone says. Without thinking I jammed my hand in between the doors to prevent them from closing. Space the person who shows up is none other than Thomas.

"What are you doing?" I ask, confused.

"I was just going to get a bit of a workout in before meetings today. There are so many meetings every single day, I can hardly get a moment to myself," he says. "What about you?"

I gesture at my own workout clothes, a pair of maroon leggings and a black tank top. He nods. The elevator ride is awkward. I've never actually spent that much time with my biological father. I'm not really sure what to say next.

An uncomfortable silence surrounds us, as he clearly doesn't know what to say either. "So how's everything going with Mom and all this?"

"What do you mean?"

"Well, I know I'm having a really hard time dealing with all this. And I don't even have to do anything important, just look pretty," I joke.

Thomas tilted his head. "That's not true. The work you're doing is just as important as everything that your mother has been doing."

Instead of responding, I just shrugged. It's not that the work I'm doing is not important, but I do feel like Thomas is just trying to placate me.

"No, really, it's true. I don't know if you realize this, but your mother talks very highly of you when you're not around." Thomas puts a hand on my shoulder and looks me in the eye. At this moment, I can definitely see the resemblance in the color of our eyes and the shape of our nose. My chest swells with pride at his words, although I'm not totally convinced that he's not just trying to make me feel better.

Well, I'm glad that somebody thinks so. I'm not really sure what I'm doing," I twine my hands together nervously. "I feel like I'm kind of just bullshitting my way through all of this." I flush at the use of such a vulgar word in front of such a formal man.

"To be honest, the rest of us are doing the exact same thing all the time. I'm not sure anyone ever truly knows what they're doing, some of us are just a lot better at bullshitting than others."

"Well," I say hesitantly, "that does make me feel a little bit better."

Thomas laughs. His shoulders shake when he laughs and the sound is a lot more booming than I would have expected from a guy like him. Sometimes I forget that he's and my mother and her other two mates basically abandoned me when I was a baby.

As that thought, I sober up. The elevator dings, opening to reveal that we have arrived on the second floor.

"I think this is where the gym is," Thomas says, gesturing to indicate that I should go first. "And really it should make you feel better, because you're honestly ten times smarter than any one of the guys we were talking to yesterday. Just because they are well known, doesn't make them smart."

My body warms at this evaluation. Who knew that my biological father was such a sweet talker. "Well, thanks," I say, as I'm not really sure what else to do or say in response.

The gym in this hotel is fairly close to the elevator, and I swipe my card to get in. I brought a pair of earbuds for my workout, but I keep them in my pocket. Instead I decide that this would be a great opportunity to learn about one of my parents. There are four of them, after all. "So, how did you and Mom meet?"

Thomas looks at me in shock, tilting his head once again. It seems like something he does a lot. "Well, it's kind of a long and weird story."

I hop on an elliptical, and wait for him to continue. He gets on the treadmill next to me and looks like he's considering his next words carefully.

"Well, you know how dragons are functionally immortal?" I nod. "Your mother and I met quite a long time ago. It was shortly after the French Revolution if I'm remembering correctly."

My mouth drops open. I'd expected that it could have been a long time ago, but I had no idea it could have possibly been that long. "Seriously?"

He nods. "Yes, seriously. It was actually in France where we met. Your mother was arguing with a restaurant owner over her bill, if you can believe it."

"Wait but haven't you guys been super rich for like forever?"

"Well, not quite. Much like you, your mother actually grew up off island. She was raised by her parents, your grandparents, but they did not want to raise her on the island for risk that she would be spoiled and out of touch." He turns up the speed on his treadmill, moving to a steady jog. "They lived on the small farm where Amelie was born. Until she was eighteen, she wasn't even aware of her royal lineage."

I frown. Nobody has ever mentioned my grandparents to me before. "I have grandparents?" I slow on the elliptical, watching for his reaction.

His face turns grim, and he sighs. "You did. They…didn't make it through the rebellion you were born into."

My heart skips a beat. I know that a rebellion happened when I was young, before I was old enough to know what was happening, but I have no idea of the extent. "Will you tell me about that? How did you guys get it to end?"

He stops the treadmill, slowing until he's no longer moving, but he doesn't look at me. It's like he can't bear it. "Serenity, you have to know that I, your mother, and everyone else wanted nothing more than to protect you. We obviously regret the decision to send you away, but—" He stops, crossing his arms over his chest and taking a moment to steady his breathing. I don't rush him. Clearly this is a difficult thing for him to say. "We did everything we could. Your mother was still recovering from childbirth when she found her parents slaughtered in their room. That day, we sent you away. It was half a decade more before we were able to end the senseless violence, and only barely."

I slow to a stop as well, waiting for him to continue.

"I'm not sure it ever ended," he admits, freezing me in place. "Many died on both sides, and we were only able to negotiate a treaty when your mother killed her own brother, the leader of the rebellion." He shivers, keeping his eyes forward. "It was horrific."

I sigh, the tension in the room palpable. "And now we're facing a new threat from the Hunters," I point out. "A dragon that none of us know anything about, other than the name Torres."

He turns to me, his face grim. "I don't think your mother would have revealed the island unless there was no other choice, Serenity. She may not talk about it, but she's frightened. We all are. When you say you're useless, I need you to understand why you're wrong about it. Honestly, you're the only hope we have left."

Nausea roils through me. I'm so exhausted from all the fighting, but I have to admit there's a certain thrill in winning. "We can fix this," I promise, my words coming out surprisingly confident. When I search myself for signs of uncertainty, I find nothing. "I need to call Jenna."

I hop off the elliptical and nod at my father, then exit the room without him. And I swear that I see pride glinting in his eyes.

Chapter Ten
Rayne

I'm trying on clothes that Gwen provided when Serenity bursts into one of the shared rooms. Her appearance startles me so badly that my hands burst into claws, and my tail sprouts from my spine painfully.

"Rayne," she says, then pauses, appraising me with her mouth agape.

I tilt my head, staying in my true form. Her tongue traces her bottom lip, and then her eyes flick back up to mine. My heart trills.

"What is it?" I ask, my voice low and soft.

She blinks twice, then her memory seems to

return. Was she really that distracted by me? "I need you for a mission. It's just you and me, and I've already cleared it with Adrian."

I frown, then reapply my glimmer so that I look almost normal. "I don't like the sound of that. Where exactly are we going?"

She sets her jaw, looking away from me as she builds up the courage to continue speaking. "We're going to my old apartment. But I need to not look like myself."

I should argue with her. Evading security in order to go to an unsecure location is a terrible idea, especially with Rebels and Hunters alike out to get her. Instead, I say, "Okay."

The apartment that Serenity used to share with two others is a shabby walk-up in Washington Heights. We take the One train the whole way, and I keep my fingers laced through Serenity's the whole way to keep her glimmer applied. She made me dress down in a pair of fashionably torn jeans and an oversized jacket, a scarf draped over my neck. Even my tattoos are covered, makeup concealing them once again. I push up the round-framed glasses as we approach the door, and Serenity swipes all the buttons.

It's uncanny seeing her so different, her body no longer tall and lithe but short and curvy, her hair a mass of brown curls. She's wearing a pair of bulky glasses, the frames thick and black, and her nose, the most distinctive part of her face, is smaller and less elegant.

The door buzzes, and we stride in, my heart pounding in my chest. Keeping up both our forms is taxing, and I find myself looking around for Torres's cronies in every crevice of the city.

We walk up the stairs, our feet far too loud on the ancient wood. Serenity stops at a door with peeling paint on the fourth floor, then pounds her fist against it. "Jenna, I know you're home," she calls. Her nose twitches as she scents the air. How long has she been doing that? I know that dragons have sensitive senses, but I wasn't aware that Serenity had learned to use hers. A shadow moves under the door, and then the locks click.

The door swings open, and a young woman with dark skin and box braids opens it, a small stone in her hand. I look closer and smirk. She keeps a witching stone handy.

"Serenity," she hisses, grabbing Serenity's hand and dragging us both into the room before slamming the door shut. Her eyes are wide as she glances to the windows, the curtains open to reveal the view of a fire escape in an alleyway. She turns to me, then, to my surprise, jabs me in the chest with a finger. "Torres is pissed you're gone, Mr. Prince Guy." Then, she goes over and closes all the curtains. As soon as she's done, I sigh and release Serenity's hand.

She turns back to normal, her hair leeching color and texture like it's draining out of her. When she's back to herself, she goes over and wraps her friend in a hug.

"It's good to see you," she breathes, and her friend, tough and angry just a moment ago, melts into a gentle embrace.

"You can't be here," Jenna replies, pulling away and resting her hands on Serenity's shoulders. She doesn't seem mad, though. A small smile plays at her lips, and she leads us over to a ratty couch. I glance at a painting on the wall, an abstract piece on canvas.

"Is this Sona Mirzaei?" I ask, pointing at the painting.

Jenna looks up, pricking an eyebrow. "Yeah," she says, surprise clear in her voice."

I let out a low whistle. "Must have cost a pretty penny."

She shakes her head. "Snagged it at an estate

sale for a hundred bucks."

I nod. Impressive. As I continue inspecting the art around the room, I realize that Jenna has a collection of hundreds of thousands of dollars worth of art. When you have connections to one of the most dangerous men on the planet, it's a good idea to have things that will be easy to sell without looking suspicious.

"Jenna, we're here for a reason. You and Greg need to get out of here."

Jenna rolls her eyes. "No shit. You're all over the news. I've got a curator coming by to unload all these paintings this afternoon, and then we're gone."

Serenity purses her lips. "Good." She looks up at me a question glimmering in her eyes, and I shrug. She looks back at Jenna. "What do you know about Torres?" she asks, clearly waiting to reveal her own information.

Jenna shrugs. "I know he's in charge of the family. I guess he's someone's uncle or cousin or something."

I cross my arms. Interesting. "You don't know your exact relation to him?" Curiosity bubbles in my chest. That seems like something this girl would be aware of.

She watches me, clearly uneasy at my presence. "I guess not," she says slowly.

I nod and back off, letting Serenity take back the lead. Jenna clearly doesn't trust me, which is understandable.

"Jenna, Torres is a dragon. We don't know anything else about him, so I was hoping we could learn more from you."

Jenna's eyebrows scrunch together, and she blinks. "I—" She clamps her mouth shut. "I don't know," she breathes after a long moment of thought. "I don't know anything about him. Just that he's someone you shouldn't piss off. Hell, I've never even spoken to him. Everything I've heard has been through the grapevine."

Serenity frowns, and I copy the expression. "Is there anyone in your family we could find out more information from?"

Jenna shakes her head, confusion lining her features. "I don't know. I don't remember." Her hands clench into fists, and her eyes water. She looks up at me, and the raw emotion stalls me. "Why don't I remember?"

I consider the question carefully. I've been at Torres's right hand for two decades, and I still barely know anything about his operation. "He uses other paranormals," I finally say. "He must have someone keeping his identity a secret. I wouldn't be surprised if he wasn't even related to you."

Jenna shakes her head. "How is that possible, though? I've known him since..." She trails off without finishing, that same confusion marring her features. Then, she shakes her head, clearing her expression. "Whatever. Greg and I will be out by the end of the day." She puts a hand back on Serenity's shoulder. "You don't have to worry about us."

They say their goodbyes, and I take Serenity's hand in mine to reapply the glimmer. We return to the hotel in silence, both of us lost in thought. The fact that nobody knows Torres's true identity bothers me. How has he kept himself so secretive for so long? Shouldn't I, of all people, know even one solid fact about him? My memories of him are a blur, and the harder I dig, the worse they get.

When we get back, the rest of Serenity's mates are waiting at the Penthouse doors. Adrian sighs with relief the instant her glimmer leeches away, rushing over to wrap her in his arms. Out of all of them, he's the most protective of her. I was honestly shocked that he didn't insist on going with me, but Serenity explained on the train ride there that it would be too conspicuous with more than two people.

"I hated every moment of that," he mumbles into her hair. I look away, the fear and vulnerability in his face far too much for me to handle. Despite being bound to Serenity, I don't truly belong with the rest of them.

As that thought crosses my mind, Dylan claps a hand on my shoulder. "Good job," he says earnestly, staring into my eyes. I give a half smile in return and remove my decorative glasses, setting them on the table beside the elevator doors.

"It was nothing," I mumble, glancing back over to Serenity for just a moment.

Dylan shakes his head. "It was dangerous. But you kept her safe in a way none of us could have."

I hesitate, then nod. The compliments make me uncomfortable, but I suppose he's telling the truth. Being able to change Serenity's appearance so completely is an invaluable skill when it comes to keeping her safe. "Thanks."

Matthew is watching me, and when I make eye contact, he gives me the slightest nod. His subtle approval is worth far more than Dylan's compliments, as he's never so much as had a conversation with me. I nod back, and he turns away.

Well, it's a start.

CHAPTER ELEVEN
MATTHEW

After Serenity spoke to Adrian this morning, he confessed to me that he still can't trust Rayne. The fact that he okayed her mission with him had come as a shock, but his palpable relief at her return explained it all. It's not like any of us really have a choice over what Serenity does. If she thinks it's best for Draecus, then there's no way to stop her. It would be easier to argue with an oncoming train than bullheaded Serenity.

Rayne slinks away after their return, and I watch him go, something about him piquing my curiosity. It could be the way he moves, or the longing look he gives Serenity before he goes. I'm half tempted to follow him, but I'd rather learn what information Serenity was able to gather about Torres. Rayne may no longer be trapped in his employ, but that doesn't make Torres less of a threat.

Serenity pulls herself out of Adrian's arms, and we all transition over to the living area of the suite. I sit in an armchair, giving plenty of room for Liam and Adrian to sit beside our mate. She looks around, her eyebrows scrunching together.

"Where's Rayne?" she asks. I gesture toward the now closed bedroom door.

She frowns. "Why?"

Adrian is the one to answer her question. "I'm not sure he particularly enjoys being around us." The disdain is clear in his voice, and I can't blame him. We found Serenity bleeding out twice after meeting Rayne in her dreams. Just because he seems to be on our side for now is meaningless when we all know that he's already hurt her in the past and could again. In fact, he could turn on any one of us.

"Rayne, out here. Now," she calls. We all look toward the door, but it doesn't open. When I look back at the couch, though, I startle, standing off my chair. Rayne is standing directly behind Serenity, a hand resting on her shoulder. His make-up is gone, and his clothes have been toned down quite a bit. Instead of a full city look, he's just wearing a black t-shirt and jeans.

"Are you alright?" he asks, his voice laced with concern and affection. I breathe out slowly through my nose before sitting back down.

She looks up at him and smiles. "Better with you here." Then, she looks at each of us, her four other mates. "As for you all, you need to calm the hell down. Rayne is with us now, and if you don't like it, the door is right there." She points at the golden elevator doors that lead from the penthouse to the lobby.

A pang of fear roils in my gut. Out of everyone, I know what it's like to be mated to Serenity but force myself to stay away. It's not something I ever want to do again, and I wouldn't wish that type of life on anyone.

I look at Rayne, whose face is pained. I sigh. "I'm sorry we've been so unyielding," I say. After everything Serenity and I have been through, I refuse to give her a reason to distrust me or ask me to leave. Adrian's hand tightens on her thigh, and he glances up at me, panic glancing on his expression for just an instant.

"You're right," he says, to me or Serenity I'm

not sure. "Our issues are our own."

Serenity's lips tighten. She shouldn't have to continue to deal with this from her mates, the men she's chosen to trust with her heart. "Good. Now, let's talk about shit that's actually important to the world."

She explains what she learned at Jenna's apartment, which is apparently very little. All she seems to know is that Torres is a mysterious dragon who uses some powerful magic to conceal his identity, which we already knew about him before. She finishes her explanation with, "At least I know Jenna is going to be safe. She took a big risk helping us in the first place."

I nod, leaning back in my seat. "What do we do with this information? Go after Torres?" My eyes flick back up to Rayne.

He sets his jaw and shakes his head. "Even without me on his side, Torres is powerful. I think it would be best to wait until we're certain we can destroy him before we take action. Anything less would be a fool's errand."

Liam chews his lip, clearly a bit uncomfortable to have the fae standing right behind him.

The queen speaks up next. "We will continue with business as usual in the US. Tomas's powers will keep us safe while we attend meetings with diplomats, and, if necessary, Henri can remove us from any truly dangerous situations." Her eyes look at each of us in turn, and I sit up a little straighter as her gaze meets mine. "Before we can destroy the hunters, we must take our home back. We cannot do that without the full powers of the world governments."

Serenity shakes her head and leans forward, seemingly unaffected by her mother's commanding presence. "Why do we even need the human governments? Doesn't it just put dragons in more danger to have the island under such heavy scrutiny?" Although we all trust the queen to know what she's doing, I'm sure we've also all had the same questions as Serenity is now asking aloud. Dragons have been separate from humanity for hundreds of years. Why are we revealing ourselves now, even if it is only in our human forms?

A twinkle lights in Amelie's eye, a smirk coming across her face. "We may be meeting with human governments, but this is only the first stage of a greater opportunity. Do you really believe that these leaders haven't been made aware of the existence of supernaturals?"

Serenity's mouth pops open. "You mean they know?"

The queen leans back and nods. "Of course.

Draecus Island may have been kept a secret, but a select few humans have always been trusted with the knowledge of our general existence. It's impossible to completely conceal the fact that dragons and werewolves and fae exist, especially in a world where everyone carries a camera in their pocket."

Serenity shakes her head. "Wait, werewolves?"

I'm not sure why that's the most surprising part of this conversation, but I laugh. "Serenity, you can't possibly think we're alone. Hell, I'm sure there are plenty of creatures that even the rest of us don't know about."

Serenity glares at me for calling her out, and I shrink just a little, although I'm still filled with amusement. "Well excuse me for being a bit new to all this." She looks back at her mother. "Okay. Then what is our actual goal with working with these people?"

Amelie explains, "Each nation has some sort of paranormal investigation agency. They communicate with different paranormal creature factions and do their best to keep them in check, as well as protect those who are eligible."

"Then why has the hunter problem grown so out of control?" Serenity demands, standing up so that she can pace. I watch her with concern.

She's been doing so much lately, and it always takes a lot out of her. What if she passes out from stress?

Something dawns on Rayne. "Because the biggest issues are in the states. Which must mean that something has changed. Even five years ago, Torres never would have attacked so many dragons in broad daylight. It was always done covertly."

Amelie points at him. "Correct." He smiles, his shoulders tense. "The United States government has done little to stop these attacks, and part of these meetings with the world government are so that we can find out what has changed. If our people are being attacked in such large numbers here, we need to know why."

Serenity sighs, clenching her fists at her sides. "Why didn't you just tell me all this before?" Frustration builds in her face, and her hands glow faintly with the heat of her inner flame. "I mean, I just met a bunch of important people, and they didn't say a word about any of it. I feel like I'm not being trusted to deal with this. If I'm supposed to take over the country someday, I need to be kept in the loop about these things."

She's not the only one surprised about the government agency thing. As I look around the room, the only ones who aren't confused about it are Amelie and her mates. Irritation swells deep in my chest. Serenity is right. She should have been notified. "I agree," I say aloud. "Keeping important information from Serenity is not a good way to handle any of this. In fact, it may have even kept her in more danger."

Amelie frowns, like she hadn't actually considered that possibility. "Alright," she says slowly. "I suppose you may be right. I will be sure to get you caught up on as much information as possible. Gwen and her mates are in the suite below us. You should make plans to study with her just like you did at the palace. There is a lot to prepare before the next meeting."

Chapter Twelve
Serenity

Our meeting with the European Union is in Luxembourg City, and the flight is egregiously long. While my mother, Phillip, and Tomas sleep in the plane's lone bedroom, Matthew and Adrian fall asleep together on the rear couch. I snap a quick photo on my phone before taking another sip of my iced coffee.

The official meeting of the EU doesn't start for a few more days, but, in the past week of studying, I've learned about an entire secret meeting that I never knew of before.

"And this?" Henri asks, showing me a photo on his iPad of an older man with tan skin, a bald head, and sagging skin.

I collapse in my seat and groan. "Herman Neuman," I say. "Head of German Paranormal Security."

Rayne sits up and looks at the man's face. "Serenity," he says gravely. My heart skips a beat, wondering if he recognizes him. Instead, he says, "This guy's name translates to Man Man New Man."

I let out an absurdly loud guffaw, startling Matthew off the couch.

Liam shakes his head. "Actually, it better translates to Mister Man New Man."

I giggle, leaning forward as laughter overtakes me. Okay, so maybe I haven't slept more than a few hours a night for the past week, but it is a hilarious name now that the guys are pointing it out to me. "Do you think he's manly?" I ask, causing Dylan to snicker while Henri rolls his eyes.

We've been on this plane for hours already, and I haven't slept a wink of that time. Gwen is passed out on another sofa, her head in Finn's lap and legs spread over Orin and Darius's laps. We still have to stop in London to fuel up before taking off to our final destination, although we won't be allowed off the plane. Overall, it will be nearly ten hours in this compressed tube with basically everyone I know.

Instead of wearing fancy clothes for the flight, I'm in the comfiest sweatpants I could find and a baggy t-shirt. Most of the others are dressed down, and it was really odd seeing my elegant mother in a pair of plaid pajama pants and a t-shirt. I would have expected her to wear one of those long silk robes, but she almost looked like a normal person in that outfit.

"When we land in Luxembourg City," Henri explains, locking his iPad, "we will be transferred to a private hotel, similar to the one in New York. It is equipped with special protections just for the meeting of the EU council on paranormals, so we should be safe there."

I stand up and move over to the armchair where Liam is reclining. It feels like I haven't been spending enough time with my mates lately, although he's been instrumental in helping me study for this event. I lean forward and press the button that reclines his leather chair. "And transport to and from the meeting?" I ask. When the chair is all the way back, I crawl on top of Liam, forcing him to scoot the tiniest bit so I can squish against his side, burying my face in his shoulder. Despite the coffee, my eyes have finally grown too heavy to resist.

"The meeting is on location," Henri explains, although his voice is getting hard to distinguish. I grunt in response, my entire body relaxing against Liam. He kisses me on the forehead, sweeping my hair back out of my face.

"Get some sleep, Princess," he whispers, his Draecus accent delectable around the words.

I grasp his shirt tightly, allowing myself to fall into a dreamless sleep.

Too soon, I'm awoken to be buckled in for our descent into London. Fueling up doesn't take long, and the moment we're back at altitude, I curl right back up in Liam's lap.
***

It's the middle of the night when we arrive in Luxembourg, the night air cool and still. Before our descent, we all changed into nicer clothing, suits specifically tailored for this trip. Matthew tied my hair in a braided updo, a skill that surprised and warmed me.

The moment we step off the plane, a placid smile on my face, cameras flash. Voices call out to us from behind the lights, begging us to answer. Instead, at the base of the stairs, my mother and I link arms and smile.

Adrian opens the limo door for us, and I take his hand as he helps me step in with my high-heeled shoes.

"God, I hate long flights," Mom says, leaning back against the limo's bench seat. "I much prefer to take portals. It's been far too long since I've been able to stretch my wings."

I nod. I haven't transformed since my confrontation with Dylan over a month ago, and the dragon inside begins to pace with unrest.

"We should fly together sometime," I say. Adrian takes my hand, and I lean my head on his shoulder.

She nods, only half listening as she mirrors my movement on Tomas, who got in the car before we were even off the plane.

The hotel isn't far from the military base in Luxembourg City, although we are led through the front door here rather than a hidden side. Cameras flash once again, and I keep my face as stoic as possible. I may be exhausted, but I'm also a princess with a duty to keep it all together. If I look even slightly off, it will be all over the news tomorrow.

We don't share a suite with my mother this time. Instead, she and her mates are on the top floor, and we're placed on the second, a split floor where Gwen stays across the hall. As soon as Adrian opens the door for me, I find myself in Dylan's arms.

"You did great," he says, holding me tightly. I don't blame him. Despite the assurances of safety, I was anxious the whole drive over that something would happen. What, I'm not sure, but there was an inkling in my gut that told me to watch out.

"Thanks," I mumble back. Before I even have to ask, Matthew is pulling my braid out, his hands gentle as he takes my hair down. I sigh. Although it's stressful dealing with all this political stuff, being in my mates' arms is worth everything else.

"We should probably get you to bed," Dylan says, lifting me into his arms before I can complain. Liam removes the shoes from my feet, placing them beside the door and locking it.

My eyes drift shut, and I sigh. "But who to choose?"

When we enter the bedroom of the suite, my eyes widen. The bed here is huge. I glance at Liam, and he smiles at the direction of my thoughts. I blush.

"Would you like to sleep, Princess?" Adrian asks, putting a finger under my chin. He lifts my face and kisses me, his lips soft.

"Do I have other options?" I breathe, and he smiles.

"Anything."

When my eyes flick over to Rayne, though, Adrian's demeanor changes. His body tenses. I look back at him, and his eyes are laced with that same tension.

"Jesus fucking…" I say, worming my way out of Dylan's arms. "Seriously?" My heart pounds in my chest as my eyes prick and heat with irritation. "You promised, Adrian. You said it would be fine."

He frowns and looks away, hurt in his expression. I take his hand and pull him toward me. "Adrian, you can't keep doing this," I say, my voice a husk. Adrian is the one who found me, the one who loved me before anyone else. His rejection of my newest mate stings like poison. A tear falls from my eye. "You keep acting like I don't know how to take care of myself, but I can. Hell, I'm more powerful than most of you." My hands heat, sparks flying out with my building anger.

Adrian's jaw ticks, and his eyes squint just a little. "He almost killed you, Serenity," he says, his voice hard.

I let a long breath out through my nose, releasing Adrian from my grasp. "I love you, Adrian. You know that. But right now, I can't be around you. Not if you're going to be like this."

With that, I turn around and stride into the bedroom. A commotion rings out behind me, Matthew's voice muttering, "Just let her be for now."

I turn to close the door, and the five of them

are watching me. "Rayne, you can join me. And everyone who trusts me to know my own damn self." My eyes don't leave Adrian's for a moment, but emotion wells in my chest.

Rayne flicks out of existence, then appears behind me and takes my hand. Dylan looks at me, then at Adrian and Matthew. Then, he looks at Liam, who sighs and follows him into the bedroom. Liam may have reservations, but he at least seems to believe me.

"Good night," I say, keeping my voice hard until I close the door. Then, a sob rips out of me, and I fall to my knees, no longer able to hold myself up.

Chapter Thirteen
Liam

I know where Adrian is coming from, but I also believe Serenity. If she chooses to trust Rayne, then I will have to trust him, too. As her chest heaves with sobs, I kneel on the floor beside her, dragging her to my chest and running my fingers through her hair.

"Why?" she asks, her hands clenching in the fabric of my shirt. I've been keeping an eye on her ever since she and Rayne were bound together, and it's clear that our distrust has taken a huge toll on her. For the past couple weeks in New York, she hasn't been eating or sleeping properly, and her eyes have semi-permanent dark bags under them. "Why can't they trust me?"

I shake my head and hold her tighter, my heart breaking with each sob. I could beat the shit out of Adrian for hurting her so badly. He's been there for her since the moment they met, but this one thing seems to be fracturing their relationship. How can he not see how much he's hurting her?

Rayne kneels down, putting a hand on her knee. Dylan sits beside him, prying one of her hands off my shirt so he can hold it.

"I should go," Rayne says, his eyes sorrowful. I've never seen him this vulnerable, and the tender way he touches Serenity adds an extra layer of respect for him.

Another sob tears out of her, and she gasps, "No, please. I can't—" A hiccup interrupts her sentence, and she doesn't even attempt to salvage it. Rayne clenches his teeth together.

Dylan is the next to speak, his voice soft. "None of us are going anywhere, Princess." He presses his lips to her hand, and I monitor her thoughts.

Perhaps it's to ensure she'll be alright, or maybe it's because I'm a masochist. Either way, what I find there is terrible. Her mind is filled with memories, horrible examples of her previous family constantly putting her needs last. Then, she thinks of Matthew abandoning her the moment we arrived on Draecus Island. I stroke her hair and tighten my arms around her, my heart racing and bile rising in my throat.

"We're right here," I mumble. "We're with you forever, whether you like it or not."

This earns a hiccuping laugh, and then another flood of tears. I stroke her back slowly, trying to encourage her to stabilize her breathing. I would hate for her to hyperventilate. "They'll get over themselves," I promise. "Really, it's just Adrian. Matthew just stayed behind to talk to him."

If I strain my ears, their voices float in past all the crying. Matthew seems stern, and Adrian is just totally broken down. I don't blame him for his feelings, but I have to admit that it's his own fault. At the moment that it mattered, he chose his pride over Serenity. Their thoughts are sheltered from me, though. They must know I would listen in.

"He will come around," I assure. I look at Rayne, who's still filled with angst over Serenity's decision for him to stay. "Perhaps some sleep will do you some good. And him."

She shakes her head. "I don't want to sleep."

I press my lips to her forehead. "Nonetheless, I think we should get you in bed. Unless you want to fall asleep on the floor."

She shudders, then allows me to lift her to standing. Her legs tremble, so I sweep her up into my arms and hold her tight. Rayne doesn't hesitate to pull back the comforter, and I rest on my knees on the mattress to lie her down. As soon as I'm sitting up in the bed beside her, she curls up against me. She's no longer sobbing, but sadness still rolls off her in waves.

Rayne takes her other side, and Dylan stands at the foot of the bed, unable to make a decision. His eyes avoid mine, and a pang shoots through my heart. How much of this hurt have I caused by avoiding Dylan in the past weeks? Every time I think that he and I might have a chance, I choose something about him that scares me off. I pat the bed beside me, and he sucks in a long and hard breath.

Are you sure? he asks with his thoughts.

I nod, and he walks around slowly, removing his dress shirt and slacks so that he lies next to me in a pair of boxer briefs and a t-shirt. I suppose I ought to change, but with Serenity clinging to me, it's hard. When I look at Rayne, I find that he's already in full pajamas. How does he do that?

I sigh and pull Serenity closer, and Rayne brushes a hand through her hair. Dylan's hand rests with hers on my waist, their fingers tied together. The voices in the next room grow quieter, although they're definitely still talking.

Before too long, Serenity's hiccuping breaths slow, and she falls asleep.

"Will you take her?" I mumble, looking at Rayne. After tonight, I resolve to never second guess Serenity's decision to trust him. I will not hurt her the way Adrian has.

He nods, pulling her gently into his arms so that I can stand up. She doesn't so much as stir, and Dylan follows to spoon her while Rayne holds her.

"I'm going to speak with Adrian," I say, a painful ball of anxiety building in my chest. This is not a conversation I want to have, but I have to. Adrian's behavior has been possessive and mistrustful for far too long, and I will not allow him to continue to harm Serenity.

ADRIAN

Why is it that I can never do the right thing? I want nothing more than Serenity's safety, but whenever I try to express it properly, I end up hurting her. First with Dylan, and now with Rayne.

Liam enters the living area of the suite, closing the bedroom door behind him with a soft click.

"How is she?" Matthew asks, sitting up straighter. I've been trying to explain my feelings to him, but the words keep coming out a jumbled mess.

Liam frowns. "Sleeping." Then, he looks at me, his eyes hard. "That's the only good news, though."

I shiver. Her sobs have dug into me like knives, each cry twisting the blades until I'm left bleeding out, and it's all my own fault.

Liam sits across from me, watching me carefully. "I need you to let me into your mind," he says.

I suck in a breath. For years, I've kept my private thoughts safe from Liam. I care for him and trust him, but my thoughts have always been my own. He knows exactly how I feel about him skimming my thoughts. It must be more serious than I thought for him to ask such a thing of me.

I nod, picturing the walls around my thoughts crumbling to dust. Immediately, Liam's presence is there, and I have to brace myself so that I don't resist this intrusion.

He closes his eyes and reaches a hand out, and

I take it. With physical contact, he'll be able to go even deeper. Maybe he'll be able to fix whatever is wrong with me, though. I just have to let him in.

After a few silent minutes of him needling around, he pulls away and opens his eyes.

"You're afraid of losing her again," he says.

I nod. Hadn't that been obvious? "When we found her on that island, I thought she was gone. She was just…empty. I can't go through that again, Liam. I really can't."

Liam shakes his head, and Matthew lays a hand on mine. I let him grip my fingers, my eyes on Liam's.

"That's not it. Out of all of us, you knew about your connection your whole life. It was like a limb had been ripped from your body when she was taken away, and you had to live with that for twenty-seven years." He pauses, glancing at the door that hides Serenity from me. "What you didn't know was that she was connected to the rest of us, and even more, that she could bond with another."

I hang my head in shame. He's right, of course. Liam is always right. "I don't mind sharing her," I say. "I really don't. But…"

The 'but' is the important part. My whole life,

I imagined finding my mate and having her all to myself. I pictured the bliss of knowing that I was special, that I was the most important thing in her life.

Liam says, "You aren't afraid of her death. You're afraid that she will leave you."

I bury my face in my hands, tears stinging at my eyes and dripping onto the woven wool rug on the floor. "I really fucked this up," I say. "I just want her to be happy, though. That's what really matters, isn't it?"

Liam nods. "It's important for us all to be happy. But I think, to do that, you need to work out your feelings of animosity toward Dylan and Rayne."

I shiver, remembering the night I woke up to find Serenity in my arms, covered in blood while her body convulsed. I go back further, reliving finding her in the woods after Matthew's death. She'd been so wrecked by their broken bond that she'd retreated inside herself, unable to come out without him. Before that, Liam had found her half-frozen in the snow. Despite how much I tried, it has never been me to bring her back from the edge. It's always the others.

Liam's face turns grim. "Adrian, without you, Serenity would not be with us at all. She almost died the night you found her. I know you're afraid that she doesn't care for you as much as the others, and it feels like she's choosing them over you."

A shudder and nausea roll through me at once. That's exactly how it feels. Maybe I shouldn't have let Liam into my mind after all. I feel completely bare in front of him, my emotions laid out on the table for him to pick apart.

"You're wrong, Adrian," he continues. "She feels as though you're rejecting her."

"But—" I start to argue, but he cuts me off with a raised hand.

"I know that's not what you mean. But by rejecting two of her mates, especially one she chose herself, you are rejecting her. You are invalidating her emotions."

He sighs and stands. "I'm going to bed. Feel free to join us if you are able to sort out your feelings on all this. If not, it's best that you don't. Because if you hurt Serenity like this again, I will have to break your nose."

With that, he leaves Matthew and I alone in the living room. I shake my head. This is a mess I created, and I'm the one who needs to fix it.

"I've seriously fucked up," I say for the hundredth time, tears streaming down my face. Liam is right, because of course he is. Still, it stings to know that I'm being a bit of a petulant child about all this. I've always been the wise, responsible leader of our group. Now, though, I feel small and stupid.

Matthew turns my face to his. "It'll be okay, Adrian," he says. "You didn't ruin anything. But I agree with Liam. I think you need to apologize and make peace with Rayne, and probably Dylan."

I let out my entire lungful of air through my nose, then nod. "You're right."

CHAPTER FOURTEEN
SERENITY

When I wake up, I desperately have to pee. The only problem is, I have to climb over several dragons and a fae just to escape the bed. My heart races when I find Adrian on the bed, but I'm careful not to wake him. Last night sends a bolt of pain through my heart, and I'm not sure if I'm ready to hear him defend his actions. I rush into the bathroom and lock myself in, taking a deep breath and evaluating myself in the mirror. I half expect my eyes to be puffy, but I look normal.

The pang from seeing Adrian doesn't leave,

and my skin shivers with cold. I turn the shower on as hot as it will go before undressing and climbing in, but my body doesn't respond well. My hands shake, and the water rushing turns to white noise while my head spins. I sit on the floor of the shower and curl forward, resting my forehead on the cool tile. I try not to think about how clean this room actually is.

My stomach lurches, and bile rises in my throat. I'm unable to stop it, and I vomit right there in the shower.

Instantaneously, another presence is under the hot water with me. Rayne may be fully dressed, but he doesn't react to the water. He only pulls me up and shoves my hair out of my face.

"Serenity, what's going on?" he asks, concern lining his features. I open my mouth to explain, but I lean forward and throw up again. "Fuck," he mumbles, holding my hair out of the way.

Eventually, when I'm gasping for every breath I can get, the nausea subsides. I lean on Rayne's chest, and he rests the back of his hand against my forehead. "I don't know what this is supposed to do," he admits, "but I think it's supposed to tell me something."

I let out a breathy laugh, burrowing my face

into his soaked white t-shirt.

"I think it's just stress," I admit. Then, I remember Adrian asleep in the next room, and my stomach flops with another wave of fear and anxiety.

Rayne wipes his hands over my face, no less concerned than before. "Are you sure you're okay?" He sounds absolutely terrified.

I nod. "I promise. I feel a lot better. Will you make me breakfast while I clean up?"

He nods, his face wary as he flashes out of the room. I stand on shaky legs, leaning my forehead against the tile wall while the steaming water cascades over me. I fumble for the hotel bar of soap, closing my eyes to keep the light from assaulting my vision while I scrub myself down. I don't have Hans's hair products with me yet, so I do nothing to my hair. He would kill me if I washed it two days in a row, anyway.

A knock sounds at the door, and my stomach does another somersault. "Serenity, are you alright?" Dylan calls, and my body relaxes again.

"I'm good," I call back. "Almost done." I rinse off quickly, then grab a towel to wrap myself in before unlocking the door.

He steps in, crinkling his nose after a quick sniff of the air. "Did someone throw up?"

Shame washes through me, and I flush. "I'm sorry. I think I was just feeling stressed about everything." A hand reaches down and cups my cheek, lifting my face so he can look in my eyes.

"You have nothing to apologize for," he says with a smile. "I'm just concerned about you."

I lean into his touch, his warmth steadying me. "Thanks," I mumble. Then, I snap out of this trance. "I should probably get dressed. Rayne is making breakfast."

Dylan smiles. "Sounds great. I'll meet you out there." I look past him into the bedroom, where Matthew and Adrian are still asleep. Liam must have already moved into the other room. I look back up at Dylan, and he gives a sad smile. "Do you want me to take you?"

I straighten my shoulders. Why should I be afraid of my own mate? He's the one who's in the wrong, after all. "I'm fine," I reply.

I stride through the room, and he sits up. I keep moving, despite him calling my name weakly. My heart stutters, but I don't freeze up. I will get through this.

"Serenity," he says again, much closer this time. I turn my face, and he's standing behind me, a hand reached out but unsure of whether to touch me or not.

"What?" I ask, keeping my voice carefully controlled to show no emotions.

He drops his hand, his eyes flickering at my tone. "I just…I'm sorry," he says.

I shake my head. "You say that a lot, but then your behavior doesn't change. Apologizing when you repeatedly act the same way isn't an apology."

He frowns, shoving his hands in his pockets. "I can be better."

I consider this for a moment. He had come to bed sometime in the night, probably after some deep soul-searching. Still, he's done this before. Hell, he didn't want me alone with Dylan until he realized that Dylan was incapable of using his powers on me.

"Show me you can be better, and I'll listen," I say. Then, I exit the room, my hands shaking.

After breakfast, Hans shows up to get me ready for the meeting with the world's paranormal agencies. He puts my hair up in a tight braided bun, and my makeup is nothing less than fierce. My suit today is dark gray with pinstripes, my shirt a deep magenta with frills around the top hem.

I am surrounded by my mates when we arrive in the secure conference room downstairs. Adrian hangs back by the doors, for which I am thankful. I'm not sure if I can be around him right now.

The room is tall and wide, a conference table stretching the whole way. Each seat has a name tag and nation's flag, although everyone here appears to be human. I sniff the air just to be sure, but I don't find any strange scents.

As soon as I enter, a middle-aged man with cropped hair and a square jaw stands up to shake my hand. "Princess Sérénité, I presume," he says, gripping my hand with a ferocity that I return in kind. "General Stephenson, Secretary of the Paranormal."

I nod, noting the American flag on his lapel.

"Nice to meet you," I say, glancing past him to see that all eyes are on me. The room is half-full at best, and my mother has yet to arrive to divert some of this attention. Several men and women introduce themselves to me, and I'm so glad for the name badges at every seat. Otherwise, I wouldn't be able to distinguish one fancily-dressed official from another.

After another ten minutes of introductions, I take my seat, opening the leather folio to go over the day's itinerary.

When a man with a German accent calls the meeting to order, I'm still alone. My mother isn't here. I send a questioning glance to Liam, who gives me the tiniest shake of his head as if to let me know he has no idea.

I take a deep breath and sit up a little straighter. If I am to be the lone representative of Draecus Island, so be it.

I expect there to be more pressing news, but, apparently, Draecus Island is the first order of business.

"When will the queen be arriving?" asks the UK member of the board. His presence is a shock to me, but Liam explained when I met him that, although this meeting is at the same time as the EU's meeting, it is a separate organization.

I shake my head. "I will be representing Draecus Island on all things. The queen had other business to attend to."

This causes a murmur to go around the table, and I sit up higher. "I assure you, I am perfectly capable of conducting my nation's business."

This shuts them up, and all eyes are on me once again. I sit as powerfully as I can, conjuring my mother's image in my head. Even though I have no idea what I'm doing, I will fake it like the best of them. At least this time I'm not the only woman in the room.

"Alright," General Stephenson says, giving me an approving smile. I don't allow my lips to twitch up from the approval, only nod back sub- tly. "First, we would all like to welcome you here. It is a pleasure to know that Draecus Island is real, and even better to understand that you are here for diplomatic reasons. We always assumed that dragons, when found out, would grow violent."

I shake my head. "A misconception. Although we have had trouble with rebellion, our people as a whole are peaceful."

I flip the page in the folio. "Now, as for some of the questions here," I say, trailing my finger down the page. "It seems that your paranormal agencies are fairly unfamiliar with dragons as a species, so I would like to enlighten you. First, we are capable of flight when in our true forms. Second, we can breathe fire, although I have yet to perfect that particular process. Many of us rely on other abilities."

Part of my studying for this meeting had been long discussions on what I can and cannot say, and I weave through the list of questions carefully. "Most clans are ruled by a matriarch, and Draecus Island is known as the origin of dragons. Although she is technically the ruler of the island, many consider my mother to be the queen of all dragons."

This causes collective looks of awe and confusion. I knew that dragons were a mystery to the outside world, but the lack of any information is absolutely astonishing. I go over as much as I can cover over the course of an hour, doing my best to stay on topic and avoid straying to information that my mother doesn't want the world to know. I don't mention what our powers are, especially not the fact that I can kill with a single touch. I also avoid discussing the lifespan of dragon kind, preferring to leave that up for interpretation. Humans tend to fear immortals, or at least anyone who lives much longer than them.

"Is being a dragon transferrable in any way, such as a bite or blood transfer?" the Polish official's translator asks.

I shake my head and smile. "No, it's something that you're born with."

Just then, my cell phone buzzes on the table beside my hand, and my eyes flick down to see my mother's name.

"Just a moment," I say politely, picking up the phone. "This is very important."

I exit the room, and my men follow me into the hall.

"Hello?" I ask, but there's only a shuffling on the other line.

After a moment, my mother's distant voice. "You will release him," she says in her authoritative tone. Her voice seems afraid, though, and something uneasy writhes inside me like a snake in my belly.

The phone shuffles again, and another familiar voice.

"You will come with us to the island." It's a voice I haven't heard in a long time, one that I had to listen to regularly back on the island.

"Feldman is here," I breathe, and my mates' eyes, all but Rayne's, widen.

"We have to leave," Matthew says, grabbing my forearm. "Now."

I nod, and they drag me through the hallways and out into the stairwell.

Voices float through the phone. "You can go

through the portal first," Feldman says. He must have forced Henri to open a portal back to Draecus Island, or possibly somewhere else in the world. I shiver as I listen to him taking my parents on the other line. There's nothing I can do, though. If they destroy the portal, then I'll have no way to follow. Otherwise, it would be too easy for me to kill them.

We can't kill Felman yet, though. Not until we know how to stop the rebels.

CHAPTER FIFTEEN
ADRIAN

Serenity still won't talk to me. After the phone call, we rush upstairs to the suite, expecting a fight. Instead, it's totally empty, no different from how we left it. Serenity keeps her face flat and stoic, packing a bag. The rest of us follow her lead.

"Where are we going to go?" Dylan asks, not really directing the question at anyone in particular.

"Anywhere," Serenity says. "It won't be long before they find us otherwise." She throws the strap of her duffel back over her shoulder and exits the room, pounding on the door across the hall. "Gwen, we're leaving. Now."

I watch as Gwen opens the door, her face filled with confusion and fear. Darius wraps an arm around her waist from behind. "Rebels are here," Serenity says. I stuff a few essentials in a back-pack, and Rayne snaps his fingers to bring every-thing he owns to him in a sensible duffel match-ing Serenity's. That must be a convenient trick.

"We need cash," I tell Gwen. "And fake IDs."

She nods, closing the door to her suite while she and her mates prepare. I wouldn't give us more than five minutes before rebels come knocking on our doors. We have to be out of the building by then, and out of the country as soon as possible.

"We're gonna have to fly," I tell Matthew grim-ly. He nods. It's going to be difficult to remain stealthy in our dragon forms, but humans who don't know about us shouldn't see anything more than birds, a convenient perk of dragon shifter powers. Still, we'll have to find somewhere spa-cious to take off. It's not like this little nation is built for dragons to shift in the middle of town.

Serenity strides back into the room, checking to make sure we're all ready. Her eyes skim over me, tearing my heart in two. I desperately want to hold her, to find out that everything is okay between us, but it clearly isn't.

I glance at Rayne, who keeps his eyes trained on our mate. The only time he's actually harmed Serenity was when he was under the control of Torres, but there's still a spike of fear that plunges into my heart when I remember how much Serenity bled that night months ago.

"Any ideas?" I ask him, doing my best to bridge the gap I've created between us.

He looks up at me, surprise written all over his face. "One. But it's kind of a last resort." I wait for him to continue, and he sighs. "We could try to hide out in the realm of fae, but if I'm found, I'll be put to death. And I'm not sure about all of you."

I ball my hands into fists. "Yeah, let's maybe make that plan E."

Rayne nods.

"What are plans A through D?" Dylan asks, hefting a bag over his own shoulder.

I grit my teeth, and we all look to Serenity. She pauses, uncertain of herself. Then, she stands up straighter and makes a decision.

"We get to the island, and we take down the rebels. Cut off the head, as it were."

So she means for us to fly back to Draecus then. If we kill Feldman, maybe the rest of the rebellion will fall apart.

"It could work," Liam says, hesitant. We all know there's more to it than that, but for now, we just need to escape.

Gwen and her mates come out of their room, and we all head to the stairwell. The elevator is too dangerous. As we exit, though, there is nothing to be found. No rebels, no danger of any kind. Instead, we are met with nothing but the emptiness of the building as meetings are well under way.

"This is too easy," Serenity mumbles when we walk out into the back alley. I nod. There's something eerie about your heart pounding from fear when nobody seems to be chasing you.

I order a couple cars on my phone, then toss the device on the ground the moment they arrive. I want to allow as little tracking as possible. Then, the vehicles drive us past city limits, then further into the country along winding European back roads.

When we seem far enough from civilization, I say, "You can let us out here." The driver seems confused and mutters obscenities about us in French. When we climb out of the car, I thank him in French as well. "I hope your day gets less strange."

The driver frowns and takes off, and the car behind us stops to let the rest of our comrades out as well.

Standing on the side of the road, I adjust my bag and start walking.

"Where are you going?" Matthew asks.

I turn to look at everyone, my hands tightening on the straps of my backpack. "This is a pretty major road. I want to get somewhere more secluded before we shift."

At that moment, everyone looks at Serenity, and her eyes tighten before she nods. "Alright. Lead the way."

We walk through the early summer heat, the fields stretching far and wide with rolling hills. I turn onto a random street, the sides lined with trees. The road here is older, less maintained than the main road we started with. After that, I turn into a copse of trees until we come across a clearing. Based on the scent of this place, humans haven't been out here in years.

Finally, as the sun peaks to indicate noon, I stop and take in our surroundings. There don't seem to be any houses nearby, and Liam shakes his head as if to confirm my suspicion. I still haven't taken down my mental walls, and it's unsettling to know that he's been in my head all this time.

"This seems as good a place as any," I say. "We should rest and then fly through the night. It'll be harder to spot us that way." I drop my bag on the ground, and the rest of them do the same. I try to make eye contact with Serenity, but she refuses to so much as look at me. "The journey is going to take a few days, and that's if we're able to fly all night. We're nearly fifteen hundred miles from Draecus Island without any portals to help us."

"I'll be picking up the things we need when we get to Bern," Gwen says, pulling a stolen hotel blanket out of her bag. She lays it across the ground, and I frown. Is she the only one of us who thought of that?

I glance at Rayne, who disappears for an instant and then reappears with a giant tent still in its store box.

"Did you steal that?" I ask, the idea of it running through me like poison. Through my years of going on dangerous missions and time being on the run, I've never resorted to theft. Shame rises on his face, but I continue, "I guess if we need it…" Admitting that he's right is less painful than I'd imagined, but I'm still not pleased that we're resorting to petty theft.

His face brightens a shade, but he's clearly just as wary of me as I am of him, albeit for different reasons. I must admit that my reception hasn't been the warmest, and I have to change that if I don't want Serenity to push me out of her life completely.

I help him set up the tent, although I don't stand too close to him. Serenity still refuses to look at me, but that doesn't matter. The fact that I can help provide her with shelter is enough for now. The tent has two sections connected by a sort of tunnel, and Gwen and her mates take one side while the rest of us are to take the other.

"Rayne," I say, his name painful in my throat. He pauses and looks at me. I hadn't realized until now that he's taller than me, but that's because I've never been willing to stand too close to him. "Would you go for a walk with me?"

He looks to Serenity, then back to me. Then, slowly, he nods.

Chapter Sixteen
Rayne

The trees are dense and cool, shading us from the summer heat. I stuff my hands in my pockets and walk beside Adrian, the one who made Serenity cry just last night. I don't blame him for not trusting me, though. Her blood is on my hands, and I did nearly kill her once. Part of the reason I don't sleep is because I'm afraid of hurting her again, only this time it would be entirely my fault.

"I haven't been kind to you," Adrian says when we've gotten out of the tent's hearing range. I open my mouth to protest, but he holds a hand up. "I just wanted to apologize. I have a lot of issues I need to work out, one of them being my jealousy."

I tilt my head. I hadn't considered that. "Jealousy?" I've assumed this whole time that all Serenity's mates care about is her safety, to the point where jealousy hadn't even crossed my mind.

He nods as we approach a stream, then sits on the edge, removing his shoes to dip his feet in the water. I copy his movement, sitting a respectable distance away from him. He doesn't speak for a long while, but I'm a patient man. I've waited far longer for far less.

After what seems like ages, he says, "I grew up thinking that I was special. That Serenity would be mine alone. When I found her, I was immediately drawn. It was like finding the other half of my soul. Then, she fell in love with the others. It made sense, because she was secretly bound to them. But…"

He turns a stone over in his hands, staring at its smooth surface before tossing it into the stream with an expert flick of his wrist. It bounces a few times before sinking to the bottom.

"But then I showed up," I finish when he doesn't. I know that my presence is an inconvenience to the rest of them. I know I'm an outsider and that I can't be trusted.

He nods. "Then you showed up," he agrees, echoing my sentiment. He tosses another stone, but this one doesn't skip. I keep my eyes on him carefully. "It made me wonder why I wasn't good enough."

I shudder. I know how he feels there. I never thought I could ever be good enough for Serenity, and the fact that she fell for me despite all the harm I've caused is a miracle. "May I say something?" I ask, leaning forward, elbows on my knees.

Adrian looks at me, his dark blonde hair glistening in the filtered sunlight. He nods.

"I'm not sure you're thinking about this the right way," I admit. "Just because Serenity was raised by humans doesn't mean she thinks like them. Perhaps it's because your parents are monogamous humans that you feel this way, but she doesn't. Serenity cares deeply for every person who cares for her." I think of the way she kissed me the first time we met in our dreams, her lips like a butterfly's wings against mine. "She can sense a good heart, and that is what matters to her. She wants nothing more than to love and be loved in return. There is no one person who could be good enough for her. And I think we all have to accept that."

Sometimes, I wish that I could have the princess all to myself. Still, I see the way she looks at her other mates, and the happiness in her eyes trills through me like a flute. Knowing that I'm on the receiving end of that type of affection is enough to keep me sane.

Adrian nods. "I guess I know what you mean."

I shrug. "And aren't you in love with another? Matthew, for one?"

He sighs and leans back on his hands. He's clearly confused about all this, but he relents, "You're right. I guess that makes me a hypocrite."

"Yes, I think it does," I say, no judgement coming through in my voice. Adrian looks at me, evaluating me. I look back at him, allowing all my emotion to rise to the surface. "I don't think I could ever be worthy of her love, but I have to try. And I think that's all any of us can do. Try."

After a while, he nods again, then stands. "I think you're right." He looks off into the woods, back the way we came. "We should probably get back and get some sleep. I'll take the first watch."

I shake my head and stand. "I don't require sleep to survive. Go to her, get some sleep, and I'll keep an eye out."

A flash of worry flickers on his face, but he

shakes it away before it can take hold. "Thanks," he says, reaching out a hand. I grasp his forearm and shake once.

"Anything for her," I say.

"Yeah," he says. "Anything for her."

An idea comes to me, so I lean forward and smirk. "So should we kiss now?"

Adrian leans back, his face turning beet red. "Excuse me?"

I chuckle and release his arm, leaning back. "It's a joke."

He looks away, the pallor of his face unchanging. "Oh. Okay."

I stride past him, putting my hands back in my pockets. "Just trying to lighten the mood."

When I glance back at him, his face is lined with amusement. We may not be close, but at least he seems less wary of me. It's a start, and it gives me hope that the rest of them might not be too far from it.

CHAPTER SEVENTEEN
SERENITY

I glide over the city soundlessly, my wings catching the air and glistening a rose gold color in the rising sun. We've only barely made it to Bern before morning, but at least there's a dragon base just south of the city where we can land. Rayne is secure on my back, and when we get close enough, he flashes from my back to the ground. I descend first, my stomach cramping as I shift into my human form just before my feet touch the ground.

I gasp and kneel on the ground, clutching my stomach. I've never been nauseated by flight before, but it's probably just stress. Rayne crouches down beside me.

"Serenity?" he asks, wrapping a blanket around me to protect my privacy.

I shake my head, unwilling to open my mouth. If I do, I'll get sick again, and that's not a very glamorous way for a princess to arrive at a new location.

An older, human woman exits the ancient estate, rushing over to me. "Princess Sérénité, are you alright?" she asks, her hands in front of her like she wants to help but has no idea what to do.

Liam lands beside me, and I would be embarrassed by his nudity if I weren't so distracted by trying to keep the bile from spewing out of my body.

"She's ill," he says, lifting me into his arms. When Matthew arrives, they have a silent conversation with their eyes. "She needs to lie down." A slight tinge of panic taints his voice, and they rush me inside, my other mates following close behind. I wrap a hand around Liam's forearm, my nails digging into his freckled skin.

"Bathroom," I gasp, and the woman opens the next hallway door. Before Liam even has the chance to set me down, I leap out of his grasp and run to the toilet. There's not much in my stomach to get rid of, but my body does its best, acid burning as it makes its way up my throat.

Matthew rubs a hand over my back, but the nausea doesn't subside like it did when I got motion sick on the boat months ago.

"I'll get you all some clean clothes," the woman says, her footsteps fading away from the crowded bathroom quickly.

The guys mumble amongst themselves, all of them clearly freaking out.

"Space," I gasp, and they back away, wary of the tone of my voice.

"Everyone move," Gwen says, her voice surprisingly powerful for her tiny frame. My mates practically leap out of the bathroom, and she walks in, dressed in a robe that seems much nicer than my blanket. She puts a hand on my forehead and drags my hair out of my face as I retch once again.

I gasp for air when nothing comes out, but my stomach is determined. I clench the sides of the toilet seat with clawed hands, shivering as my body desperately tries to rid me of whatever the hell is wrong.

"I think the stress is getting to you," Gwen mumbles, tying my hair back in a ponytail holder that she somehow procured. I nod, resting my forehead against the toilet seat and breathing slowly through my nose. She looks up, and I follow her gaze to the five men staring at us. She frowns. "Can you all be useful? Adrian, find a bed. Rayne and Liam, food. Something bland as hell. Dylan, go get cold water and some ibuprofen. Matthew, clothes, for Christ's sake."

They all snap into action, and the room feels far less claustrophobic.

I take in deep breaths, and Gwen rubs circles over my back. "You'll be alright," she says, her voice far more calm and confident than any of the guys had been. I nod, slowly to avoid startling my body into another puking fit. "Have you eaten anything strange? Did something stress you out when we arrived?"

I shake my head. "I don't think so," I croak, my stomach rumbling with a sudden hunger as though there's nothing wrong. "I got sick yesterday, too."

Gwen sits back on her heels, an arm wrapped around her knees. She frowns. "It could just be extreme stress from everything going on. Or…"

I lift my head. "Or?"

She frowns, then stands up to lean against the sink. I'm not confident in my ability to stand quite yet. She watches me, waiting a moment before speaking. "When was your last period?"

I roll my eyes and open my mouth to speak, but then close it again. After a moment, I whisper, "Gwen, I'm not pregnant."

Her eyes narrow as she keeps her eyes on me. "Are you certain? What form of birth control have you been using?"

I snap my mouth shut, heat rising in my face. My whole life, I've been a stickler about birth control, but with my mates, it hasn't crossed my mind even once. I consider it for a moment, putting my hands on my lower stomach and feeling nothing but hunger. "Matthew would have known. He's been checking me every day."

She chews her bottom lip, considering my words for a long while. "Unless..." She stops, then restarts. "Do anyone's powers work on Rayne? You already know that Liam can't read his mind, and Adrian can't sense his aura."

I let out a too-loud guffaw. "You can't be serious. That would be—"

"A normal response to unprotected sex," Gwen interrupts. "I'm glad you agree."

I sit up and cross my arms over my chest, but I know there's a chance she could be right. A big chance, if I'm being honest with myself. It's not as though I've been at all careful with my mates.

With everything going on, an unexpected pregnancy had been the last thing on my mind. "What am I supposed to do?" I ask, fear lacing my voice and betraying me. I put a hand on my stomach again, wondering if she's right.

She sighs. "I'll get you some pregnancy tests, to start. You don't want to tell them and be wrong. I have to go into the city for the rest of our supplies anyway. Just try to relax and get some rest, alright?"

I nod, and Adrian rounds the corner at the same time as Rayne. "We got you a room," Adrian says, now somewhat dressed in a pair of sweatpants and socks. Rayne walks over with a bowl of chicken and rice.

"Thanks," I say, and he helps me up with his free arm. Adrian doesn't so much as twitch at the physical contact between us, which is a marked improvement. My legs wobble when I stand, and Adrian takes the bowl so that Rayne can scoop me into his arms.

"Lead the way," Rayne says, following Adrian through the hallways until we reach a brightly lit bedroom with the standard giant bed to fit me and my mates. The supernatural world may be stressful, but at least I don't have to choose which mate to share my bed with, unlike human accommodations.

Rayne sits me up, and Adrian hands me the bowl. Shortly after, the rest find me, all clothed again. That's good, at least. I'm not sure I'd be able to concentrate knowing that my mates were all walking around with their dicks out.

"This is a nice house," I say, avoiding eye contact with everyone. I can't help but think about what Gwen said. I might be carrying a baby, and Rayne may be the biological father. Will Adrian and the others react badly to that? I glance up at Liam, who seems puzzled but not shocked. Clearly, he still can't hear any of my thoughts about Rayne. Will that change when the baby comes? I shake my head. I don't even know if I'm pregnant. It could all just be a false alarm. My symptoms match extreme stress as well, so I'm not going to rule that out.

Rayne sits on the bed with me, and Adrian joins on the other side, although he doesn't quite touch me. My heart longs to reach out to him, but I still don't know if he's changed. He and Rayne talked yesterday, and they seemed amiable when they returned, but that could just be a momentary thing. I have to be extra careful in case…

No. I have more pressing things to think about right now than a possible but improbable pregnancy. Can fae and dragons even have children together?

I shovel some of the food into my mouth. It's super bland, but my stomach thanks me for it nonetheless.

"Are you feeling any better?" Adrian asks quietly, and I nod, my mouth full of food.

"Could be sleep deprivation," I say, half hoping to convince myself. He doesn't seem convinced, but he doesn't press the issue. I wonder how long it will take Gwen to get me a pregnancy test—or maybe five.

"I think we all need some sleep," Matthew says, collapsing on the bed on Adrian's other side. I hand off my now-empty bowl to Rayne, who sets it on the bedside table. Then, I lie down and close my eyes.

Chapter Eighteen
Serenity

It's late afternoon when I awaken alone. I sit up and take in my surroundings, blinking away the sleep from my eyes. This is the first time I've slept more than a few hours in quite a while, and I feel far more refreshed than I would have expected.

I dress myself in the leggings and t-shirt laid at the foot of the bed and pad out of the room, listening for any indication of where my mates could be. My stomach rumbles, so I wander down and follow my nose to the kitchen. Rayne is standing with his back to me, shirtless as he frosts a bunch of cupcakes.

"That's a fantastic sight," I say, licking my lips. He turns around and smiles, his eyes tense.

"How do you feel?" he asks at the same moment my stomach grumbles loudly. He relaxes a single degree, and I stride over, grabbing a chocolate cupcake off the plate. I unwrap it slowly before taking a careful bite. His baking skills are absolutely divine, and I want to savor every bite. "Shouldn't you eat something bland?"

I roll my eyes. "If you try to take this from me I might have to stab you."

He chuckles, watching me consume the dessert with care. When I'm finished, he leans toward me, his tongue running against my upper lip and sending a shock through me.

"You had some frosting," he says, then presses his lips to mine. I set the cupcake wrapper on the counter and wrap my arms around him, taking his slow kisses as they come. His hands move to my hips, and, as though I'm made of little more than air, he lifts me onto the counter.

I groan and open my legs, allowing him to step in between them. I wrap my legs around him, tightening my grip on his neck and deepening the kiss. I take his bottom lip between my teeth and bite down gently, and a groan comes out of his throat.

A knock sounds at the door, and Rayne jerks away from me like I'm on fire. I clench my hands into fists against my thighs and slide off the counter, looking toward our intruder.

Gwen stands there, her face red with embarrassment at the interruption. "I was hoping to have a moment with Serenity," she says.

My heart skips a beat. For just a moment, I forgot about the possibility that I might be pregnant. And if I'm not, what the hell am I doing about to have more unprotected sex in this random kitchen? Have I learned nothing at all?

"Of course," I say, following her out of the room and shooting Rayne an apologetic look. He offers me a half smile and goes back to frosting his cupcakes.

Gwen leads me to a bathroom, handing me a box out of her messenger bag. I swallow my nerves and go in the bathroom alone, reading the instructions. I've never had to take a pregnancy test before, and the fact that I actually have to pee on one end is off-putting. Gwen bought me a three pack of tests, so I use all of them in one go. Even if one is wrong, two out of three will be enough to tell me if I should see a doctor.

After I replace the caps and wash my hands, I open the door for Gwen to join me. I'm nauseous, not from whatever has been plaguing me lately, but anxiety. What do I do if I am pregnant? Am I actually ready to be a mom? If it's Rayne's baby, what will happen? A fae and dragon baby would surely have some genetic abnormalities.

"Serenity, breathe," Gwen says, placing her hands on my shoulders. I suck in a breath, tears stinging at my eyes. Her face remains steady, though. "It is going to be alright. I promise."

I take a steadying breath and nod. "How long are these things supposed to take?"

Gwen checks the time on her watch, which she must have picked up today since none of us can have phones for fear of being tracked. "Five minutes. It's been three."

I nod, crossing my arms over my stomach. If I'm pregnant, wouldn't I have felt something? There isn't so much as a twitch, though. I close my eyes and breathe, waiting for the time to expire.

Gwen reaches past me and gasps. I snap my eyes open, and her mouth is open in shock.

I look at the tests on the counter. All three of

them have the same result.

Positive.

I thought I would freak out when I found out, panic about the implications. Instead, I rest my hands on my lower stomach, a small smile playing at my lips as the tension releases from my body. Perhaps my fear had been the unknown, the possibility of it going one way or another.

Gwen watches me for a moment, then pulls me into a hug. "Congratulations," she says, her joy clear in her tone. When she pulls away, I'm full-on grinning. I'm going to be a mom. That's such a strange thought. Motherhood is something I've never really considered for myself, but the knowledge that I'm growing a life inside me feels so right.

After a moment, though, reality sets in. We're in the middle of a war. Not only that, but the only reason Matthew wouldn't have sensed the pregnancy would be because the baby is half fae. I keep a hand on my skin, taking a deep breath.

"Gwen," I say, and she looks up at me. "Don't tell anyone."

Her eyes widen. "I'm not sure that's a good idea."

I shake my head. "If it's Rayne's, then I'd be

eight weeks along at the absolute most. I don't want to mention it in case…"

Her lips tighten into a thin line, and she nods in understanding. "You don't have to say anything else. I'll keep it quiet for now." She hesitates before speaking again. "Do you think it's wise for you to continue with your plan in this condition?"

I sigh and shake my head. "I don't have any choice. It's not just me who will be affected if I don't go back to Draecus Island. It's hundreds of thousands of people. Including my parents. We have to try. And I'm the best chance we've got. Nobody else can bring people back from the dead, after all."

Gwen cracks a half smile and opens the door, stuffing the positive tests back in the box and then burying them in her bag.

"Thanks," I say, filling my voice with all the gratitude I can muster. "For everything. Remind me to give you a raise when we get back," I joke.

She chuckles. "Of course. I'll hold you to that."

We fly out the moment darkness falls on the city. I keep trying to figure out what's going on with Serenity, but her thoughts just seem blank. Does her mysterious illness have something to do with Rayne? I brush the tip of my wing against hers as we soar through the night, a gentle keen pouring out of my throat.

Are you okay? she asks using the telepathic link all dragons share in our true forms.

I'm alright. Just concerned for you, I reply. Rayne is riding on her back once again, holding on tight. *Perhaps someone else should carry him if you're feel-*

ing unwell, I suggest.

She doesn't reply for a moment, her eyes ahead as we coast through the cool night, stars above and city lights below. *That might be a good idea for tomorrow night*, she eventually concedes.

The rest of the flight is calm and quiet, occasional conversations here and there to keep us organized. For the most part, though, it's quiet, all of us focused on what we have to do.

Just before dawn breaks, we land in Latina, a town just south of Rome. It's our last stop before we are to arrive on Draecus Island, and we have to stock up.

Serenity doesn't vomit again when we land, although it's clear that she's feeling ill the moment she shifts back. I cover her in a loose-fitting knit dress before putting on my own pair of sweatpants and t-shirt, and she shivers and braces herself against whatever it is she's feeling.

"Let's get you inside," I say, leading her to the small cottage owned by the Queen. It's usually only occupied a few weeks a year, although it is well maintained and cleaned regularly. The building is squat with a red Spanish Tile roof, and the whole thing is only made up of two bedrooms, each with their own bathroom, a small living area, and a kitchen.

Serenity walks straight to the master bedroom after Adrian points it out to her, and her hand brushes his arm when she exits. We all notice it, but nobody says anything.

"I'm going to make some breakfast," I say just to avoid having a conversation about all the tension in our group. I put on a pair of slip-on sandals and grab the keys off the hook in the kitchen, then go out to the garage where a short, inconspicuous coupe is parked.

As the garage door is opening, the passenger door to the car opens, and Dylan joins me. I open my mouth to protest, then close it again. If he wants to go with me, I'm not going to stop him. It's not worth the argument, and, if I'm being honest, his presence is almost comforting.

I find the nearest grocery store on the car's GPS, then put it in gear and tear out of the dirt driveway.

"Do you have any idea what's wrong with her?" Dylan asks. I glance over, and he's staring right at me.

I shake my head. "I'm not sure," I admit. "It's kind of torture."

Dylan sighs. "Worst mind reader ever," he jokes, leaning his head back and opening his window. The summer heat billows in, quickly overpowering the car's air conditioning.

"I mean, you're a killer who isn't allowed to kill anyone, so you're one to talk," I jab back. I've never made light of Dylan's terrible, addictive power before, and the moment the words are out of my mouth, I regret them.

Instead of getting angry with me, though, he laughs. His voice is light and easy, and I glance over to find his golden hair glistening with the early morning sun. The wind tosses it around and makes it messy, and I crave the idea of running my fingers through it to adjust it. Despite my discomfort with Dylan ever since he started using his powers again, I can't help but want him.

"It's a nice day out," he says. "Pretty weird considering we're about to go into a war zone."

I nod as everything comes back into perspective. I'm under no illusion that the night is going to be easy, and I fear that we might not all survive. My stomach flops, and I clench my hands tighter on the steering wheel.

"With all of us together, we should be able to defeat the rebels. Or, at the very least, we can rescue the queen and try to take out Feldman." The name of the general who betrayed his people leaves a sour taste in my mouth. Despite weeks with him in council meetings, I hadn't been able to sense his defeat, and that alone unsettles me.

Dylan puts his hand on the passenger mirror, his tendons and veins standing stark against his skin. I have to stare at the road ahead to keep myself from getting distracted, and I force myself to stay away from his thoughts. Feeling the way he wants to kill makes me sick, and I'm not sure I can handle it right now. When my mind subconsciously digs at his, though, I don't find that darkness inside. Instead, he's thinking about the trip to the grocery store. He's picturing taking my hand, going around the side of the building, pushing me against a wall, pressing his lips to mine,—

"Jesus Christ, watch the fucking road," Dylan says, grabbing the wheel as I apparently try to swerve into oncoming traffic. I snap back to myself, narrowly avoiding hitting a young woman on a motorbike headed the opposite direction. My entire body is alive with fire, and my face heats with embarrassment.

"Sorry," I mumble, my knuckles going white against the wheel. I grit my teeth and count the seconds, forcing myself to focus on driving and nothing else.

"I'm sorry," Dylan replies. "I guess you probably noticed what I was thinking about."

I nod, swallowing the panic rising in my throat. Is that something Dylan actually wants? I don't know how long I've wanted something to happen between us, but all the emotions involved rose right back to the surface when I got just a glimpse of his mind.

"It's fine," I force. I pull into the lot of the grocery store, and, to my dismay, the sign is still flipped to Closed. It makes sense. It's not even six in the morning yet. I rest my hands in my lap and keep my eyes forward, my face hot and probably scorching red with embarrassment.

Dylan lets out a long, forceful breath through his nose, then turns to face me. "Are you pissed at me?" he asks.

My face snaps to look at him, and his eyebrows are tilted down as his face fills with distress. "Of course not," I say. His expression doesn't change, though. I take a short glimpse at his surface thoughts, and the wind is knocked out of me. I slump my shoulders. "You think I hate you." It's not a question. His thoughts are far too clear for that.

He chews his bottom lip for a moment before replying, "Well, you've been avoiding me for kind of a while."

I nod and look out the windshield. There aren't

any other cars out and about. We really did leave the house too early. We probably should have gone to sleep and then woken up to eat. Instead, I'm waiting in a parking lot being forced to confront my feelings.

"Your power frightens me," I admit. "Sometimes, I wonder if you could kill one of us."

Dylan sighs. "I get it. Sometimes I wonder that myself."

A memory flashes through me, something I haven't thought about for quite a long time. It was the dead of night, and we were all asleep in our own rooms of a condo in Los Angeles. We were on a mission to find a young human-born dragon, and Dylan had insisted on bringing his girlfriend, Siobhan. She'd been perky and excitable, desperate to join our team.

I was awoken to a cry of absolute anguish that rang through me like a siren, and I sprinted through the halls to find Dylan in his room. Siobhan, once so full of glee and life, was nothing more than an empty shell in his desperate arms. Sometime in his sleep, they'd touched, and Dylan's powers had sucked the life out of her before either of them knew what was happening.

I don't look at Dylan, but I lay my hand over his on the center console. He's clearly remembering the same thing, and his eyes well with tears. Siobhan may not have been his mate, but he did love her. His love for her had burned so bright that his magic destroyed her in a desperate attempt to have her closer.

"I'm sorry," I whisper.

He shakes his head. "It was a long time ago." His voice is gruff, though, and out of the corner of my eye, tears glisten on his cheeks.

I lean toward him, resting my head on his shoulder. His hand tightens in mine, and he lets out a sigh as all the sadness flows out of him.

"I'm sorry for avoiding you," I say. "I do trust you. With the bond, I'm not sure you'd be able to hurt any of us." I breathe in his scent, and my heart pounds at our closeness.

"Liam," Dylan whispers, his Irish accent lilting over my name the way it was meant to be said. I lift my head and look at him, and his eyes flick down to my lips.

Before he can say anything else, I lean forward, crashing my lips against his with the full force of everything we've left unsaid between us. The hand I'm not holding reaches up and cups my cheek before he bites my lip, and I return the favor by using my free hand to pull his hair, his head tilting back so I can bite the crook of his neck.

Kissing Dylan is a battle, our wills butting against each others' in a desperate clash of raw hunger and emotion. Dylan's hands turn to claws, the tips digging into my skin. I allow myself to partially shift, my teeth grazing along his throat and leaving tiny dotted trails of blood.

He growls against me, his hand tightening on my cheek and dragging my face away so his golden eyes can stare into mine. Right now, he's absolutely terrifying. His features are drawn and sharp, and there's something animal about the way he evaluates me with those slitted eyes. I pant as he watches me, and I realize that he is absolutely stunning.

Too soon, though, movement outside catches my attention. A middle-aged man is approaching the shop door, and he unlocks it before flipping the sign to "Open."

Dylan bares his teeth, his top lip curling as my attention is stolen away from him.

I put a hand on his face, my thumb tracing over his bottom lip as I shift back into my fully human form.

"We'll finish this later," I promise.

With a frustrated sigh, he changes back.

CHAPTER TWENTY
SERENITY

The final flight is tense and utterly silent. We go faster than ever before, darting through the night like phantoms. For a moment, I think of the Night Witches, an all-female Russian bomber group from World War II. They would shut their engines down and dive to drop their bombs, starting the engines again mid-air so they could go home.

If we aren't that stealthy, then we have little hope of winning.

The darkness envelopes us, the stars hidden by thick clouds. Thunder rumbles above us, and my body thrums with lightning.

Liam is carrying Rayne tonight, the only sound the flapping of Rayne's clothes. I breathe in the familiar scent of the island before it's even in sight. When I see the outline, my heart calls out.

Home. I'm home.

There's something ominous about it now, though. The city doesn't have a single light on, and there are no boats in the harbor. As we draw closer, I inspect the streets for any sign of movement, but there's nothing. Not so much as a leave blowing across the road in the still night air.

We descend on the castle, Liam leading us as we circle down. My senses are on high alert, even the slightest sound like an assault on my ears. Memories of the last attack of the island are like a barrage. It had been daytime, and dragons had plummeted into the sky in a desperation to escape.

We each land silently on the highest tower, dressing in dark gray as quickly as we can. If someone isn't looking closely, we might at least blend in with the stone walls.

Dylan opens the door, and I catch him clenching his shaking hands. He knows that he may have to kill tonight, and it's already affecting him. I place a hand on his shoulder, and fear is in his eyes when he looks at me. He doesn't want to lose control again.

I give him a short nod, and he responds in kind.

We have to focus. We don't know who's in the castle or how many there are.

Liam leads the way, his footsteps lithe as he descends the pitch-black staircase. We don't dare use any flashlights for fear of being caught.

I don't know how I know my mother is here, but something in my soul is telling me I have to be at the castle. Feldman could have been talking about any island on the phone, but I know that this is where it's happening. Draecus Island is where it all started, and this is where he wants the rebellion to end.

I stay shifted enough to see, ignoring the cramping in my gut that I get every time I shift back into my human form now. The dragoness inside me coils for a fight, and I think about the life growing inside me. I can't bear the idea of bringing it into this world in the middle of a war. My child will be safe.

We come out in the hall, and we all strain our ears. Liam looks back at me, his eyebrows scrunched in confusion. He must not hear any-one.

Still, I know that we aren't alone. Goosebumps

rise on my skin as we sneak through the halls, as light on our feet as possible.

Rayne flashes out of existence. With his experience as a mercenary, he's able to search the castle more quickly than if the rest of us were to do it on foot.

He returns after a few moments, shaking his head.

I grit my teeth. How can it be that nobody is here? I can feel it deep inside me. Something in this castle is calling to me, yet there's nothing? There's not even evidence of the battle from months ago. In fact, it looks entirely normal. Like nothing ever happened.

As we push the ornate doors open for the throne room, the great hall where we've held every event, something in the air crackles and shifts. My eyes can't seem to focus on anything, and the paintings and tapestries on the walls go from normal to torn and ragged in a moment. The hairs on the back of my neck raise, but my vision keeps slipping off the throne at the head of the room.

I rub my eyes and look to my men, who are equally confused.

One by one, the ancient sconces along the walls light, flame burning a pale blue, hot as can be. As each flame comes to light, so does a figure beneath each.

When the front of the room is lit up, there's a man standing with his hand on the back of my mother's head. Her clothes are ragged and her hair is a mess, but she seems unharmed.

"Feldman, let her go," I say, my voice strong as I stand up straighter and take a step toward him.

"Serenity, something isn't right," Adrian mumbles, but I ignore his words. Beside Feldman are three more men, each with one of my mother's mates. A knife is pressed to the throat of each one.

My mother tries to speak, but her voice is nothing but a wisp of air. They've taken it somehow, just like they did at the ceremony. If she's silenced, she can't use her power of command.

"You should leave, Princess," Feldman says, his knife flashing in the dim light. His face is drawn and inhuman, a few scales glinting on his temples. His nostrils flare as he takes in our scent.

I take another step forward.

"You know what I can do," I say, keeping calm. "Let them go, and we can work out a way for you to get out of here alive."

He lets out a burst of laughter, and the shadow in the throne behind him shifts. I shake my head, white noise blocking me from thinking about that shape too hard.

"You think you can still win this?" he asks, a dot of blood dripping onto the knife. My mother gasps, but she doesn't attempt to move. Her eyes are wide, her teeth gritted as she stares at me.

I look around the room, the rebels stiff and motionless between the lights. Some of them have claws, and others have guns.

Rayne puts a hand on my shoulder, rock hard and stopping me from taking another step. I glance at him, but he's staring at one of the figures in the shadows.

"That girl," he says. I look closer, but my eyes must be deceiving me. The short-haired person he's staring at may be holding a gun, but she's just a teenager.

A human teenager.

"What the fuck?" I breathe, my eyes flicking over to Rayne.

He reaches out, his palm up. "Winry," he says, a warning evident in his voice.

How does he know her name? As I look around the room again, though, the sense of dread pulls my eyes away from the throne.

That's when it snaps into place.

"You're working with the Hunters," I say to Feldman. My voice is careful and measured, but my insides are utter turmoil.

Feldman laughs again. "Not exactly."

I grit my teeth. "Torres, show yourself," I demand. "Stop the hiding, stop with the games."

The shadow on the throne moves again, a dark chuckle reverberating throughout the room.

"You are not my concern, Princess," he says. "The only qualm I have with you is that you stole what belongs to me."

Rayne's hand tightens on my shoulder, and I reach up to grab it.

"You can't own anyone," I say, my voice ringing out through the room and slicing through the tension in the air.

Torres comes into the light, but his face is still unclear. At least I can look at him straight on now without my mind slipping every few seconds.

"I think you'll find that you're wrong," he says, his voice silky as a venomous snake.

I brace myself for an attack, but it doesn't come. Torres just stands there, watching us. Waiting for us to slip up.

"Why do you hide your identity?" I ask. I don't actually know how I'm going to approach when he's so slippery. Last time we faced him, he disappeared in his full dragon form. If I'm not careful, I could hurt my mom.

The darkness fades from his face like a shadow receding, revealing the face of a man in his early forties. His hair is long and dark blonde speckled with gray, and he has lines from age. For a dragon to show any sign of aging, he must be absolutely ancient. My blood runs cold as my own eyes stare back into mine.

My mother looks up, gasping, "No. You can't be here."

I watch the interaction, my limbs going numb.

"Taranis," Henri barks upon seeing his face. His eyes are wide with terror. "You're dead. I saw you die."

Torres—or Taranis, as Henri is calling him— shakes his head, his hair glistening from the lamps. Something in this interaction draws my breath out of me. "Did you? Or have you forgotten my power?"

With a wave of his hand, realization dawns on all my parents' faces. Tears spring from my mother's eyes, falling freely down her face.

"You killed them. You tore our parents' throat out," she says, her voice still a complete husk.

That's when it clicks, my mind far too slow. Torres is Amelie's brother. My uncle.

I straighten my spine despite every nerve in my body screaming at me to run. "Why do you kill dragons when you're so desperate to rule them?" I demand.

He raises an eyebrow and turns back to face me. "Nobody has to know who I killed," he says. "In fact, I could be the prince returned from the dead. The leader of a new world, one where dragons take their rightful place at the top."

Bile rises in my throat. He'd led the rebellion when I was born, and possibly many more. Mom has said this wasn't the first time there were issues with rebellion.

"How many?" I ask, my hands sparking with violet rage. I picture the people who've died, think of the families that I couldn't save.

He shrugs. "After a while, you lose count. Did you know my parents disowned me so that Amelie could rule? The moment she was born, they loved her more." His words are casual, like he's given this speech a thousand times before and it doesn't matter.

Mom shakes her head. "That's not true. You know it's not. You were lost far before I came along. It just took me for them to realize it. That's why they left to raise me."

Taranis blinks, glancing at her like he forgot she was there. General Feldman still has his knife, and it presses harder into my mom's neck when she tries to speak.

"I do wonder," Taranis muses, looking back to me and tilting his head.

I wait for him to speak again, but when the silence stretches, I bark, "What?"

He smiles. "What wounds can you heal?"

It's like the world turns to slow motion. His hand reaches down, gripping my mother's hair and stealing the knife from Feldman's hand. As I take my first step to run, he swings, and the blade slices through her flesh, far deeper than should be possible.

It goes clean through, and the room explodes into sound.

"Amelie!" Tomas screams, jolting out of his captor's arms as if he can do anything to save his mate.

Taranis smiles as her body falls, his hand still in her hair, her gaze distant and faded.

I sprint forward, ready to grab Taranis and drain every bit of life out of him. Instead, he disappears, my mother's head falling to the ground. Feldman lets out a single burst of laughter, his eyes alight with excitement as he sends flames through her body.

He doesn't flee fast enough, though. I grab his fiery hand, and instead of taking his life away quickly, I let every bit of it sink into me, relishing the feeling of electricity as it stings my body.

He screams, and the hunters look around, ready to move forward. The girl Rayne pointed out takes a shaky step forward, her gun barely held up. Rayne isn't even looking at her, and I'm about to scream his name when Adrian dives at her, grabbing the gun out of her hands. He doesn't kill her, though, for which I'm thankful. She's just a kid, after all.

Feldman continues to scream, but the rest of the room is too involved to give him a second thought. My mates, Gwen, and her mates all burst into action, taking out every hunter and rebel in the room.

Feldman may not have seen what his forces were, but the moment it was revealed that he was working with Taranis, I knew. They are nothing more than fodder, bodies to count at the end of the day.

The last of his life force flows into me, and I kneel beside my mother. I can't look at her, though. I put a hand on her, but with her body in flames and her head detached, the life force built up inside me has nowhere to go. The rebels holding Henri and Phillip look at each other before releasing them. Then, they run, disappearing through a doorway.

The screaming doesn't end, and Tomas can't even put his hands on my mother's body.

Taranis fled, but it was only because he knew he'd won.

Feldman is dead, and so is the dragon rebellion.

My mother is dead, too.

Cut off the head, and the rest comes tumbling down.

CHAPTER TWENTY-ONE
ADRIAN

I do not cry.

Life filters back to the island slowly. First are the soldiers, those that Gwen knows are loyal to the crown. Phillip gets into gear instantly, although his eyes are hollow. He's never without Henri and Tomas, and they do everything in their power to stay standing.

Witches are hired to redo the spells on the island that were destroyed by the invasion months ago. They work relentlessly to keep us safe. The outside world is no longer allowed in. No cameras, no reporters, nothing. It's like the island never really existed.

Matthew does not cry.

He gets to work healing those wounds that need healing, and he does his best to balance the chemicals in the minds of Serenity's fathers. They are needed for the time, and they know they have to be strong.

Matthew knows better than any of us how it can feel to be torn away from a mate, although it had been his death to take him away. His hadn't been permanent, just an inconvenience, really. Serenity spent hours trying to mend her mother, far longer than anyone else was willing. There's no fixing that type of death, though.

The castle is cleaned up bit by bit. Without the rebellions' spells concealing them, the true damage had come to light. Walls were blown out, wall hangings were destroyed, rooms were torn apart. It takes a while, but with enough help, we're able to get it all done. Countless ancient relics are lost, but the structure still stands proud against the horizon.

Dylan does not cry.

After dispatching several rebels and hunters, he was confined to Serenity's chambers. He'd been so filled with death and blood that he couldn't be trusted around the workers trying to get the palace put back together. Instead, he plans the funeral in isolation. All decisions are made through Gwen over video call or through the doorway. With a week to decompress, he should grow safer to be around.

A funeral for a dragon queen is no easy feat, but he takes it all on his own. He even goes so far as to contact the vendors as civilians return to the island.

Liam does not cry.

He and I work together day and night to vet each returning citizen. It's exhausting, but it's absolutely necessary. With our powers combined, it's easy to ensure that none of them are rebels, come to destroy us once again.

Serenity does not cry.

She walks the castle grounds day and night, consoling anyone who seems to need it despite the wall of agony that is her aura. Her face is calm and kind, though, and everyone has what they need. She goes to meetings with the council, trying those who were complicit in the rebellion and the queen's murder.

She holds her head high, her judgements swift and vicious. At night, she falls asleep quickly. Due to everything going on, I'm unable to spend much other time with her. Gwen and Rayne assure me she's doing well, although they're very obviously concerned about her.

SERENITY

The day of the funeral is hot, the sun shining gold and pink on the horizon past the west end of the island. I've never been out of the palace, but it turns out there's life all over this place. There's even a small village out here, the stones of the streets even older than those that construct the palace.

I am dressed in the traditional white of dragon mourning, the color of snow in a dreadful winter. My gown falls to the stone of the ceremonial cliff, snagging against the rough designs carved into it in the language of dragons. I should ask Adrian to teach me that someday, or maybe Liam or Matthew.

My fathers stand beside me, their faces as stiff and unmoving as the rocky cliffs. Waves crash down below, and my mother's body lays under a white silk sheet on a pyre.

Thousands are gathered behind us, my men among the foremost people. They're all in white suits, and Rayne's tattoos stand out like ink on a canvas. He explained to me that the demon tattoo on his hand was Taranis's symbol, well known in the paranormal community. It's also on a tapestry in my mother's office. I must have seen it every day back before all this and never realized where it came from.

A woman sings in my peoples' language, her voice trilling over the cliff and into the wind. The song is sad, I suppose. Appropriate for the funeral of an ancient one. Considering how long dragons live, my mother died quite young.

Died. She's dead.

Sometimes, I half expect to see her walking with one of her mates, but she isn't there. The stark reminder that she's well and truly gone hits me like a punch to the gut every single time, knocking the wind out of me.

After the song ends, the woman leads me to the pyre, and I hold my hand out, a small wisp of flame licking my fingers. I rest it on the wood and kindling, and it lights slowly. Henri goes next, his eyes on the form below the sheet. Then it's Tomas's turn, and then Phillip's.

I keep my hand there, letting the flame burn away every emotion in my body. When I pull away, I do not feel.

Eventually, the crowd dissipates. Nobody wants to see the grand funeral pyre of a queen fall to a smolder.

I stay, though, watching every bit of flame until there is nothing but ash.

Then, Adrian steps forward, kneeling in the ash and ruining his white suit. He grabs the only surviving object from the coals, a glistening golden crown.

The only ones left are my fathers, my mates, Gwen, and her mates. They are the only ones to watch as Adrian takes the ash crown, placing it on my head as I kneel. When I stand and look to the ocean, the sun disappears over the horizon.

"May I announce Queen Sérénité Amalia Claudette," Adrian says, although there is no gusto to it. There is no applause, no amazement. It's just me and my loved ones, and none of us can find joy in this moment. This is not how it was supposed to be.

I take Adrian's hand, staring out at the horizon.

"Let's fly," I say, releasing him so that I can dive off the cliff.

I am the Queen of Dragons, and I will have my revenge.

To be continued...

Keep reading for a preview of Dragon Queen, the thrilling conclusion to the Draecus Clan saga!

CHAPTER ONE
SERENITY

The cliffs are the only place where I feel alive. I stand over the crashing waves, the wind forcing my hair to fly around me, the wet strands whipping my skin and leaving red marks with the force. My black mourning robe hugs my otherwise bare body, the chiffon hazy. A storm tears around me, but I am still as a statue.

I have a long day ahead of me, but I can't help but come out here every morning. Lightning crashes into the horizon, the sea glowing for just an instant.

My bare toes grip the very edge of the rocky

face. An inch forward, and I would be falling. I close my eyes and release the robe, my alabaster skin bright against the darkness of a rainy dawn. The rain caresses my skin, and I fall forward, plunging off the cliff.

Just before I hit the water, my body transforms, the dragon inside forcing her way out. I slice through the black sea, the water ice against my rose-gold scales. I arc through, my breath warm in my lungs while the child in my belly rolls at the shift.

I pump my wings once, breaching over the crashing waves. Many humans would be afraid of what could be hiding in these murky waters, but I am the most fearsome thing out here. Perhaps the most fearsome thing anywhere. I pump my wings again, lifting myself from the water. Thunder crashes around as the sky goes white again, and a rumble grows in my throat.

I should return to the palace, but the summer storm barraging me from every side is filled with the same sweet destruction that roils inside. My body twirls through the air of its own accord, and every thought that's been haunting me for weeks flies out like the raindrops I shake off my scales.

Too soon, though, a bronze dragon descends from the island, his body coiled with ropy muscles.

I thought I might find you out here, Dylan says through our telepathic connection that only exists in our true forms.

I sigh, a low growl releasing with it. Are you stalking me?

He lets out a dragonly laugh that shakes the air around us, tilting his wings so they brush over mine. We have work to do. Meetings to attend and all that fun stuff.

My upper lip raises over my teeth before I can stop myself. Why are there meetings when the world is falling apart? Why do I have to pretend that nothing is wrong when my mother is dead?

Dylan dips down over me and nips at the raised spinal ridges on my back, and I twist my head to snap at him. It's too late, though, and he's careening away with a laugh.

I adore him, as I do all my mates, but he really knows how to piss me off. I dive after him, clamping my teeth down on his tail and dragging him down to the sea.

I surrender, he shouts with a laugh in my mind just as we plummet into the sea. He yelps, bubbles bursting from his mouth as the water chills him to the bone. I release him and pull myself out of the water, then tilt my body back toward the island. I know he's right, of course. Draecus Island is in absolute shambles, and I am the one who's supposed to fix it. Now that I'm queen, everyone looks to me to know what to do.

If only they believed in me. Most of them give me uncertain glances, worry dotting their expressions. Amelie, my mother, was supposed to have more time. It wasn't supposed to be like this. But, just like he killed their parents, Taranis killed his sister.

I'm gonna get you back for that, Dylan growls, a shiver running through him as he flies beside me.

We land on the highest tower, shifting simultaneously as we reach the familiar stone outcropping where we've landed countless times before. I place a hand on my slightly bulging stomach, a smile coming to my face as my baby moves. Around the same time that started happening, I stopped vomiting with every shift. I absolutely won't miss that part of pregnancy.

Dylan and I dress in the stairwell landing where we've started to stash clothes as of late. Before I pull my shirt down, he rests a hand on my belly, a faint smile coming to his lips as he feels the life moving inside me.

"I think Dylan the Second is a great name," he

breathes.

I slap his hand away and huff. "Absolutely not," I say for what must be the millionth time. For weeks, my mates have been arguing over the name of the baby. They were initially pissed when they found out I went into battle pregnant, but that anger was far outweighed by worry when they realized I'm carrying a half-fae baby.

Matthew was the first to realize the baby's parentage. He'd attempted to inspect me and determine the baby's health, but he couldn't sense anything from my womb even after a blood test proved that I was definitely pregnant.

"I'm choosing the name," I insist. "You all can choose for later kids, but I have dibs on this one."

Dylan's face lights up with excitement. "We're having more?"

I roll my eyes and tuck my shirt into my black slacks, then slip on a pair of low-rise heels. "I need you all to stay occupied somehow while I'm running a country. I'm thinking of a one-one ratio. That way nobody gets jealous that they aren't holding a kid."

His grin brightens a few more degrees. "So there might be a Dylan Junior?"

I roll my eyes. "I still get veto power. No juniors, no sports guys, no joke names."

Dylan snorts. "Okay, but Fyre Byrne was an actually awful idea."

I shake my head and tie my hair up in a tight bun as we walk down the circular staircase. "Okay, everyone except Adrian gets to name one. Fyre Byrne is probably the worst name idea in history."

We come out in the hall, and the smile slides off my face. My mother's portrait is on the wall right across from the secret stairway entrance, and my heart skips a beat. This is the only way I'll see her anymore, but there's so much I need to ask. I may have my mates to support me, but the moment I discovered my pregnancy, I imagined my mother holding my hand through the delivery.

Dylan puts an arm around my shoulder and pulls me in so he can kiss my forehead. "It's okay to be sad," he mumbles, and I blink away tears.

"I'll be alright," I say just as Gwen turns the nearest corner, her hair tied back as she strides toward me in stiletto pumps that still leave her inches shorter than me.

"Your majesty," she says sternly, "you have a meeting in ten minutes with the council."

I sigh and nod. "Of course," I say, straightening my back and following her. She rattles off information, and Dylan leaves us be as we approach the council chambers. Liam is there waiting for me, as always. I lean up and give him a peck on the lips, and he smiles against me before pressing our foreheads together, his eyes staring into mine.

Gwen clears her throat, and I pull away from him. "Yes, of course," I say, guards opening the doors for me. Having someone else open every door takes some getting used to, and I still find myself reaching for the intricately-carved mahogany from time to time.

The chatter in the room halts the moment I stride in. The men and women of the council watch me, wary. I frown. They've all been walking on eggshells around me like I could explode at any time. Despite my entire life falling apart in a matter of months, I'd like to think I'm handling this all pretty well.

About the Author

ALEXIS PIERCE *is a small-town writer with a big-city heart.* She travels the world full time in search of a place to call home, and, when she's not writing about sexy supernatural creatures, can be found spending time with her husband and dogs.